Light Reading

Reflections in Poetry and Prose

Also by Beth Richards

Reflections in Verse :
ISBN: 0-7223 3578-4,
Arthur H Stockwell, 2005

Chill Out With Beth :
Gems for Young and Old!
ISBN: 0-595-37203-1
iUniverse 2005

W O W: Words of Wisdom
ISBN: 0-595-40724-2
iUniverse 2006

Journey Towards a Dream
A Novel
ISBN: 0-595-42834-7
IUniverse 2007

Worlds Apart
Poems of Contrast
by Beth Richards & Charles Muller
ISBN: 0-595-50302-0
iUniverse 2008

Light Reading

Reflections in Poetry and Prose

Beth Richards

DIADEM BOOKS

Published by Diadem Books

For information, please contact:

Diadem Books
Ocean Surf
CLASHNESSIE
IV27 4JF
Scotland UK

www.diadembooks.com

Cover painting by Beth Richards ('Baccaro Lighthouse', in oils)

ISBN: 978-0-9559852-9-4

Acknowledgements

My thanks are due to my Husband and friends for all their encouragement—also for the support they've given me during the six months or so it took me to compile *Light Reading*.

Without them and also the inspiration that I consider came to me from God, I could not have achieved the end result.

There is a poem in the poetry section entitled 'They Say'—one of the sayings is simple and appropriate here: "It's better to give than to receive."

So I give you *Light Reading* in the sincere hope that you'll receive it and read it. I hope that it will be well read!

Beth.

Foreword

I first began writing poetry way back in the last Century, some forty years ago. But it wasn't until I retired that I began to be serious about it—and then only because of three things.

Firstly, I had more "me" time on my hands. Secondly, I had the encouragement of my husband—and, last but not least, I found a very good friend and Publisher who really encouraged me to continue.

For this, my fourth book of poetry, I've included some "free verse"—and because I've enjoyed venturing into writing short stories I decided to make this a compilation book of the two subjects.

I was also fortunate in persuading Charles Muller that it would be a good idea if we compiled a book of our poetry works together. This we did, and because of the differences in our writing and subjects, we named it, very appropriately, *Worlds Apart*. Although we are two very different people who have led very different lives, we worked well together, and are very much 'Kindred Spirits'.

Now, everyone always says that each of us has at least one novel in us somewhere. I'm no exception, so I wrote my novel, which was published last year (2007), entitled *Journey Towards a Dream*.

I've always maintained that writing poetry (and other forms of creative writing) is a gift from God, and although I said after my joint effort with Charles, "That's it, I'm laying down my pen," I think that God doesn't agree with me—for here I am, still writing very earnestly! Hence this latest book of short stories and poetry entitled *Light Reading*. (Discerning readers will, of course, appreciate the pun on the word *Light*, hopefully made clearer by my oil painting of the Baccaro Lighthouse on the front cover! In case you don't know, Baccaro Lighthouse stands on Baccaro Point, close to the southern end of Nova Scotia.)

I really enjoy writing 'free verse', and so there are quite a number of these in this latest book of mine. It appears to come frequently and naturally to me. This way I'm able to delve into my subconscious and reflect some of my innermost thoughts.

I certainly believe that if one is blessed with a gift of any kind, one should use it. I believe that mine are Gifts from God.

Beth Richards

Part I

Reflections in Poetry

Table of Contents: Poems

Baccaro Point Lighthouse

Thy Word is a lamp to my feet, a light to my path.... Psalm 119:105.

The lighthouse stands there – upright
Silhouetted against the ebony of night.
It's the saviour for all shipping ploughing
watery furrows in the gigantic ocean,
a welcome or forbidding beacon of light –
to ships and vessels as they are tossed and thrown
about on roller-coaster waves.
On a foggy night the warning wails
penetrate the sightless gloom.
This beacon of light, forbidding them to advance
too close to the jagged rocks that lie below.
This beacon, welcoming, its light beams out,
a sign of hope to any vessel that's been drifting
perhaps for seeming aeons of time in a watery world,
the first sighting of life it has glimpsed in such a long while.

See this light,
Shining bright,
In the darkness of the night!

No Man is an Island,
But the Lighthouse stands there erect and alone
on its plinth of rocks, its own Island!

We all have our guiding light, whether it be Jesus—

Thou rulest the raging of the sea.
When the waves thereof arise,
Thou stillest them...
(Psalm 89:9)

—or just someone that we admire...

Baccaro Point Lighthouse is just one of many dotted all around the world,
Saving the lives of seamen with their warning sirens, crying out into the
night.
Its light beams to any ship that might advance towards the dangerous rocks,
hidden in the thunderous waves below…

Some Lighthouses are manned by men who live in desolation to help others;
Baccaro Point Lighthouse, now automated, still calls out to living souls.

The sea has many moods, at times tranquil, but can rage in torrents with
waves rising to a height of 30ft. or more! What chance would any ship stand
in a torrent like this without the warning lighthouse, for the sea is like a giant
tossing a toy around, shaking it like a rag doll. Just like anger totally out of
control.

Even Neptune tried to rule the waves, to no avail—but…
The Lord on high is mightier than the noise of many waters: yea,
Than the mighty waves of the sea. (Psalm 93)

Light can have many meanings, for instance…
Just like the Lighthouse, it can light your way.
To a lover—'You are the light of my life!'
To reflect hope—'The light at the end of the tunnel!'
To relax—'Lighten up!'
Even a candle gives candlelight.

A candle burns bright,
It gives out a glow of light,
A warm and radiant sight,
Is candlelight…

'Eddystone Lighthouse' (also Smeaton's Tower)

The first Eddystone Lighthouse – Henry Winstanley's construction – was
erected in 1695, but was washed away seven years later, along with
Winstanley. The second lighthouse to stand on the Eddystone Reef, thus
John Rudyerd's lighthouse, was completed in 1711 but was burned down in
1755, so not long standing!
In 1882 the present Eddystone lighthouse was built, and stands now fourteen
miles south of Plymouth Sound; this was built by Sir James Douglass.

However, on the mainland, visible from the sea, is Plymouth Hoe with Smeaton's Tower quite dominant in position there.

It was constructed by John Smeaton (thus named Smeaton's Tower) in 1759, and is now a main tourist attraction on Plymouth Hoe where it was re-erected in 1884. The entire section above the spiral staircase is original. Smeaton's construction originally boasted twenty-four candles as a warning to any vessels of the dangerous reef. The rock below the Tower was undermined by the sea, the lighthouse was demolished— but its stump still remains beside Douglass' Lighthouse, the current Eddystone Lighthouse, on an adjoining rock.

For thou wilt light my candle;
The Lord my God will enlighten my darkness....
(Psalm 18:4)

The Lighthouse is a house of great power; it determines the path of many vessels out on the high seas. It sends out signals of dangerous waters and rocks.

Lighthouses are like our windmills dotted around the country, that stand proud, erect and regally against the backdrop of the sky.

The waters saw thee, O God,
The waters saw thee-- they were afraid;
The depths also were troubled...
(Psalm 77:16)

12/8/2008

A Day at the Hospital

Are this country's services going downwards?
I'm asking this to see if you agree?
Are you feeling like me?
'Cause many of my friends do, not just me!

To visit a hospital these days, you need much to take along with you,
A good size handbag for starters, also a purse for change,
As parking the car is no longer free!

That's if you can find a parking space,
Which incidentally is like an obstacle race;
You join a queue,
Your appointment's nearly due,
Because it's taken you,
So long to park, and that's true!

You think you're there
With time to spare,
These obstacles happen, do we care?
'Course we do, but it's very rare,
For things to get better.

You then, follow the arrows to where you have to go,
You book yourself in, then wait in the row!
They trot back and forth
For all it's worth.
You sit and patiently wait,
You think to yourself, I might as well have been late!
Your appointment time is now, well overdue,
For it appears everyone's called, except you!
So after an age, you go and enquire
Why am I waiting, have I been forgot?
Often the answer is no, we have not!

When you do get your turn, even that's not the end,
As it will then depend
If you need a prescription, my friend.
It's a visit to the pharmacy, if you do.
Another surprise then awaits you,
YES, again there's a queue!
Hours later, you can at last go home,
For many of us, this is an escape for today,
Hooray!!
But how long before we go back another day?
We're led to believe things are better than in the past,
What improvements are they, and will they last?

If you're unlucky enough to be kept in overnight,
Yes, that's what I said, that's right,
When the nice doctor discharges you, at maybe 9 a.m. next morning,
Here's a dour warning,
It could take hours to be free,
So if you're lucky, you'll maybe get home in time for tea!

14/6/2008

A Dream—or Nightmare?

It was only a dream!
Or so it would seem,
but the reality of it so great
I felt I was there
and awoke with a sense of morbid fear!

It was therefore 'a nightmare'
so terrifying I was actually there
again, all those years ago.
Saying "goodbye" on a railway station,
broken hearted,
soon to be parted,
you and I, for a while that loomed as though forever.

Such a lengthy time apart
until we'd be together again 'sweetheart'.

I touched your face softly
so that I'd recapture the warmth of you
on another day too.

A day when you'd not be there,
I whispered a prayer,
to keep you safe
until you were back home again.

Then I awoke, and thankfully, you were lying there beside me,
and to my relief
I knew it was just a dream,
a dream that has haunted me through the years.
But it was so vivid
That it really did seem
So real!

23/9/2008

A Heartfelt Plea

Many years ago my late Father-in-Law lived miles away.

Two hundred and fifty to be precise,
I so hated that journey
because it wasn't nice!

Besides, I wasn't too keen on him either,
maybe it was a mutual feeling,
as sometimes he'd hit the ceiling
when we made an excuse at the very last
not to visit.

However, now that's all in the past.

I realised for the first time today
just why he'd say
the things about us that he did,
for what goes around,
comes around.

We now live many miles away from our family, and find it hard to accept
their lack of enthusiasm to visit !

For you see, we're getting old ourselves now,
we want them to show
they care about us,
and so disappointment is at the heart of the matter!
We look forward to a visit
and when it doesn't happen,
we take it to heart.

So that's probably what happened in the past with Father-in-Law,
but we were too young to understand.

We hurt him!
And now it's payback time for us.

With age comes understanding and wise thoughts.

It's too late to do anything about how we treated my Father-in-Law,
BUT I just hope that our family will understand how we feel
Before it's too late…

22/9/2008

Anger...

Why do I get to feel so angry?
It doesn't help anything, but...
it's buried deep inside me.

Is there any escape or hope that I may
feel different one day?
In some way?

I know the source of my angry feelings,
but know that there are no easy solutions;
sometimes this worries me
as I do not have a violent nature.

I deal with these feelings the only way I know how!
I write, I paint, I play relaxing music.
Is this all that I can do?
I've searched my mind,
but fail to find,
an answer of any kind.

Somehow I have to sever the cord of discontent.
Cut myself free from the core of this anguish and pain.
Everything else I've tried in the past, to no avail!
Forget the existence of those closest to my heart.
Hard to do, but somehow I must try, for my sake and the person I love.

I so wanted love, and what have I got?
Rebellion, someone close to me who's hard and has no feeling it seems.
Normality is what I crave
but it's only going to be in my dreams!

15/6/2008

Autumn in England

The early dawn chorus the birds treat us to has ceased.
The mornings and evenings are quite dark.
Trees are losing their summer abundance of leaves
as they fall and gently drift to the ground.

Remaining shrubs and bushes have turned a burnished gold
and vibrant red
instead
of the lush greens of summer.

The gentle breeze that strengthened into gale force winds overnight
stripped those autumn leaves
and threw them to the ground.
Which in turn is now covered in swirling leaves of burnished gold and
vibrant red.

The only leftovers now are the berries,
winter food for the wild birds,
those left behind after the summer migrants have flown.

Even the cobwebs are transformed,
hanging in mid-air as they do with droplets of moisture
clinging.

This all occurs between the heat of long summer days
and the cold dark chill of winter.

Cottages in the countryside can be seen—at this time of year
with twists of smoke spiralling towards the skyline.

In a very short while our nights will turn colder.
And that moisture now clinging to the cobwebs
will be frost—clinging like limpets to the tree branches,
resembling hairy spiders' legs!.

This is England in autumn,

17/10/2008

Bank Holiday Madness

Why have I been sitting here musing for the past two hours?
I'll tell you why!

Everything's ground to a standstill. Yes! We're all sitting here on the
Motorway,
going nowhere just now.

You could say, 'we're all in the same boat!'
Except that we're not!
We're in our cars, waiting to move.

We're all heading for a destination to somewhere!
So why do we put ourselves through this stress?
Because of our stressful lives, we try to get away for a break from all the
routine,
The workplace,
The school run,
Shopping—one hundred and one things we all do daily to make a living.

But is it worth it, looking around me?
Drivers, families,
Fractious kids asking
When are we going to get there, Dad?

Is this mayhem, hold up, caused by some selfish driver who's caused an
accident somewhere probably miles away?
If it is, then someone may not be going anywhere, except perhaps a little
earlier into the next world.
The tailback must now be several miles long.

Ah-ha, soon we begin to move slowly, at a crawl,
We are off to Porthcawl,
On our way at last!
We've been there in the past,.
It'll be worth it in the end,
My friend.
We'll get down to the beach,
It'll be within our reach.

This weekend is a bank holiday,
The reason so many go away
And stay!
Just for a few days, before once more,
We'll be heading back home, to work, school, reality.

Let's pray we get back safe and sound.

23/8/2008

Blood...or the lack of...

When names were given out
I should have been allotted—Stone!
Why? Because getting blood out of me
Is very hard to be done!

I'm off today, three samples they want,
I hope my blessed arm doesn't say it can't
part with it today!
I'll just sit and pray, for come what may,
They need it anyway.

I sit there while she pokes and prods.
Will it come out?
That's in the lap of the Gods!

Her sense of humour was pretty thin,
not a grimace or a grin,
when I asked about a transfusion perhaps?

Three whole bottles, it wasn't much I wanted to know,
I haven't much to show,
just a bruise and aching limb.
I ask her what happens now?
She glances up with a furrowed brow,
Just phone and they'll let you know
the results.

So that is it for this fine day.
In the meantime I sit back and pray,
that I'll hear from them when they say,

With luck you'll live another day.

17/9/2008

Chalk and Cheese

What is the difference between thee and me?
Quite a lot really, some of it you can't see.
But there is plenty!

Why do we get attracted to our opposites?
It's easy when you think about it; it's so simple,
It's all about envy!

The quiet, shy person, would so love to be like his counterpart,
who is so outgoing and sociable, and
although it's envy, it's sometimes—nice envy !
Really like 'chalk and cheese'
Total opposites.

People who are sensitive often envy those who appear hard.
Those who appear hard and can't show their feelings, and
those who are unfeeling, may wish they could bare their soul.
But they can't, because
they can't let go!.
If only they could.

They can't let anyone into their secret haven,
For fear of what they might find.

The larger, fat, rotund person, is very often attracted to the thin person.
Why is this ?
Mainly because they dream of having an hourglass figure!

Children are probably the biggest copycats of all.
A quiet child will often pal up with a loud type, because that's what he
dreams he'd love to be.

So can you begin to see?
The difference now, between thee and me?

I for one, am different to my other half,
I love music,
he likes music, but that's not the same as me,
he lacks my passion for it.
I couldn't live without music! It does something for me,
it relaxes me when I'm stressed.
Our difference might be because I can play the piano,
and my other half can't,
so maybe that's the reason for the difference between us,
it could be another type of envy.

I once had a very good friend who lived in a very untidy, disorganized home.
I am totally the opposite, for I couldn't live like that!
Things have to be neat and tidy and well organized with me,
but how I envied my friend, who could live, and be happy in her disorganized way.

    I really do know the difference between thee and me!
    It's a matter of 'Chalk and Cheese'.

30/5/2008

Contentment...

Contentment is being happy with your lot!
Happy with what you've got.

It comes from within,
it cannot be bought.
Give it some thought!

It means not wanting or craving anything material.
Does that sound—surreal?
It's not meant to.

Now happiness CAN be bought.
A gift maybe that you desire,
it'll set your being on fire.
But only for a short while.

Whereas "contentment" is an inner glow.
I should know.
For I am totally blessed,
for I am both happy and contented,
it's really heaven sent
and not just lent
for a while.

I have peace of mind
which can be very hard to find.

But "contentment" brings you this,
this feeling of inner bliss.

This inner glow, straight from the heart.
It makes you feel good.
The feel-good factor.
Everyone is chasing the feel-good factor.
But I have it!
So be it!
This is it.

In one word – "Contentment"…

18/10/2008

Do As I Say, Not As I Do...

What is a dictator?
Someone who rules by force.
Do as I say, and not as I do!
Has this been said to you?

It's really bullying, and often begins in the school playground,
By someone who's bigger than you!

How does anyone stand up to a Giant?
Do not assume or accept that you can't!

Show an outward bluff, look your opponent in the eye,
And whatever,
Don't show fear, or
all will be lost,
at any cost.

Stand up for yourself with pride
However you may tremble inside.
This kind of small dictator is someone we've all met at some time in life.

But throughout the world today there are Dictators,
Those who rule by force,
And of course,
Millions suffer at their hands.

Why does anyone want power by means of force?
Because,
In the end,
My friend,
Just remember...

The meek will inherit the earth...

11/8/2008

BETH RICHARDS

Global Warming

What's happened to our weather?
Do you remember in years gone by
when we'd have a whole day of blue, blue, sky?
Nowadays, we just don't get two days alike.

In bygone days our winters were cold.
Jack Frost would pay a visit overnight, and
paint our windows, with lacy patterns, ne'er
two patterns would be alike.

No central heating in those days,
no double glazing either,
so the icy pattern would be inside the windows as well as outside.

Germs and bugs didn't stand a chance of survival!
In winter, in the cold iciness, large icicles would hang suspended from
gutters,
just like giant frozen fish!
Tree branches, thick and furry looking, covered in whiteness,
snow several feet deep in the rural countryside,
skating on the village pond!
The rivers would freeze over.
Even the sea would freeze at times!

We had four seasons way back then.
Now it's hard to distinguish our seasons by the weather, as
March can bring warmth, just like a summer's day now!
Whereas a day in August, can appear to be like a day of winter gloom.

Why the change in climate?
They tell us it's down to this thing called

'Global Warming'…

21/6/2008

It Makes You Think

A stroll along the sandy beach in the bracing air,
with my dogs racing back and forth, diving into the rolling waves that
wash towards the shoreline.
The piercing cry of the seagulls overhead, as they plunge like jets into the sea
for food.

All this on a morning stroll,
the sky now blue with the sun glinting,
dazzling bright after the previous night of torrential rain and raging storms.

I bend down to pick up a piece of driftwood, tossed on the beach –
probably from last night's storm and hurl it back into the water for my dogs
to retrieve.
Exercise for them and pleasure for me, so wonderful,
at no cost in terms of money.
But money can't buy that kind of pleasure!
But it's often the small things in life that can be so precious.

Especially to someone who's been through a life-threatening illness,
a time when you didn't know if there'd be another tomorrow for you?
So always enjoy any small, precious moment, as if it were your last,
because we're not immortal any of us.

So many people take life and each new day for granted,
but life is God's gift to us at birth and taken back one day.

I'm thinking these thoughts today as a person who's life could have been
snuffed out like a candle.
But this time is wasn't, and I've been spared.
But how long for?....
That is in the lap of the Gods, for all of us, the length of time.
However long it might be,
make the most of each new day,
Just as I do…

9/9/2008

Kindred Spirits

Our paths crossed because of our love for the written word, yet I feel that I
know you well.
Just like our Heavenly Father, through some of my in-depth 'free verse', you
know my innermost thoughts.
We have conversed on the telephone at times, so
by listening to your voice I can tell, you have warmth, also
a great depth of feeling inside.
Like myself, we are kindred spirits because of our love of painting, and
our love for things of beauty. I too have a great love of music, and could not
envisage life without it!
Through writing and poetry, also with encouragement from you I feel that
I've reached a summit that I might not have achieved without your help and
compliments upon the way.
I trust your judgement in this sphere, and I love it when I can feel trust in
someone.
Just like our joint venture with it's title 'Worlds Apart', we are at the present
time— just that, 'Worlds Apart'. Yet looking at the moon, as many
thousands have done in the past, and will continue to do so in the future, no
doubt, we are united at least in the mind at times.
I'll probably not stop writing, as it's in my blood and no doubt I'll ask for
your opinion again sometime in the future.
We two, really are 'Worlds Apart'—you with your doctorates, me with
nothing to speak of educationally. All I have is any wisdom I have learned
during a lifetime.
I've always maintained that destiny plays a large part in our lives.
It was through destiny (your advert in Saga mag!) that our paths crossed, and
I'm so pleased that they did.

From your kindred spirit, Beth. 12/5/2008.

Memories of Bygone Days

I won't speak your name, only in my mind, but you're now gone away, so very far.
I can never reach you now, never again, only in my mind.
What we had was special, it wasn't true love, but a kind of lust, an addiction, just like a drug!
Whenever you were troubled, you would come to me.
I'd listen and try to pour oil on troubled waters.
We were mates, I was very fond of you. I believe at times you fancied me in your mind!
I think I always knew this anyway.
Firstly we were both free when we met, but went on to meet and marry different partners.
But contact remained because of circumstances and through our lives we were mates, friends and finally drawn together with a chemistry, and that's entirely what it was—
Chemistry!
But while it lasted, it was good.
Distance separated us finally, but we kept in touch and remained friends.
I think back often to times spent together with loving thoughts.

12/5/2008

Memories to Treasure

Animals can give so much pleasure,
also pain!
They are like the weather—
it can rain.
My dog left memories to treasure,
so many memories, that I could never love again!

Unconditional love they give
all the time they live.

Now I borrow from a friend.
For I know that at the end,
no tears and pain will I endure.

My neighbour has a Ginger Tom,
although his visits are constant,
he has his uses,
so I've no excuses.
for chasing him off now and again.
as he entertains as well as being an intruder.

But he *will* sit waiting for the birds—that makes me cross!
But he couldn't care a toss!
Is he the boss?

There are frogs under my garden rocks,
he just looks and cocks,
his head in total confusion…
I find this very amusing!
Suddenly he'll pounce, but miss the frog
who then hops it, under a log!.

A grey furry creature did come to grief,
it was beyond belief !
I watched this show as 'Tom' crept stealthily on his belly,
but unlike the frog, the mouse wasn't quick
and after tossing and playing with his prey,
off 'Tom' went home that day
and I had to clear away
the skeleton of the mouse!
But thankfully it wasn't in the house.

No doubt 'Tom' will be back again,
but at least I won't feel the pain
if he gets run over by a passing car.

I'll just miss the amusing antics,
the shows he gave to me,
for Free...

20/10/2008

Musical Power

I've just been lifted by a piece of music,
right out of this earthly realm to somewhere high above.
From this magical move
can I prove
that above all else, the power of music surely comes from above!

The power of music is unquestionably strong
and can lift you out of your mood;
it never lacks to amaze,
it pilots us to another Kingdom way above
which is good.

It has a healing power, so strong
it can lift someone from out of a coma
by playing constantly their favourite song.

Music is really poetry
translated to rhythm by a musician,
sometimes orchestral, sometimes vocal,
sometimes in a foreign language,
sometimes local..

Whether it be pop, classical or jazz,
country and western, even a hymn maybe,
it will appeal to someone,
It's universal,
controversial,
relaxing, healing,
it'll always be appealing,
to someone.

I love music and can't visualize life without it,
it touches my emotions,
so much so,
that I can completely let go,
and drift into another world,
just for a while,
I can lie back and smile.

It can make you rejoice,
just by listening to a voice,
you make your own choice,
of what it is you listen to,
but I guarantee,
whatever you may choose,
it will surely get through,
to your heart.

For there's nothing to compare to good music!

22/9/2008

My Belief is This...

Where do we go to when we leave this planet earth?
For what it may be worth
I have my own beliefs on this, but whether they may be true,
I'll leave others to decide.
In our skies at night,
Millions of stars shine bright.
Somewhere out there in the vast black atmosphere there must be something,
other planets maybe!
Who knows?

All I feel in my heart goes back to when my Father died, to
the moment he ceased breathing.
I knew then that the man who'd been my earthly Father was no longer there
inside the body lying there before me.
That body was now just an empty shell.
Something was missing!
What was it I wondered?
I believe it was his soul.
We all have a soul,
But where does it go to when we die?
I believe it floats way up high,
Into the sky,
To another planet somewhere, another life maybe!

So I am not sad anymore when I think of him, for if I am correct then surely
we'll meet again one day and this is only a temporary parting.
In my heart of hearts I cannot believe that this life on earth is all there is.

There has to be something else somewhere!
Or are we re-born in the future like a plant? For in the winter it appears to die
and then when spring arrives again that plant will burst forth into life.

For what it may be worth,
This is what I believe happens when we leave this earth.

26/3/2008

"Jesus said, I am the resurrection and the life: he that believes in me, though he were dead, yet shall he live: and whoever lives and believes in me shall never die. Do you believe this?" John 11:25, 26

My Loss...

My voice is just an echo in the wilderness,
crying out in anguish!
Where are you?
Already I am missing those special moments of contact,
those shared confidences,
words that mean so much.
You're special, and someone as special as you –doesn't come along
everyday.
All I can say
is—it'll be good when you're no longer away,
out in space.

In my mind I can picture your face.
but still I seek contact again.
It's lonely and empty, I am all alone,
just me—on my own.
I treasure your words of encouragement and compliments.
To me they mean so much.
Just being able to keep in touch.

It's the unknown that I fear most,
it makes my whole being feel lost.
I really don't know why,
but we're Kindred Spirits—you and I.

My inspiration has faded into oblivion,
because my guiding star has disappeared from view.
Even the moon is sheltering behind the cloud tonight,
also gone from sight.
So I cannot even say goodnight—
what a plight!

You've become my good friend,
and my mentor, I've learned so much from you.
and that is true.
Your epitome of words, so descriptive,
so invaluable!
It's like being on a one-to-one basis with a teacher.

My path to writing has surpassed my own expectations,
because of your close interest in my progress.

The climax of my day,
will be—when I hear you say
you're back home again to stay.

Stay happy.
Stay safe.
That's my prayer from me to you.
Just for you.

23/10/2008

My Prayer...*

Please, please, please, Lord, don't ask more of me than I can give!
I want to live.
I want to be alive.
I need my sight,
I want to write.
Please help me to cope and get through this bad time.
At the moment I can't see any light, or beacon at the end of this long dark tunnel.
No ray of hope even...
I need love and support,
I'm lucky with earthly support,
please fill my being with heavenly support.
I don't want to feel alone, just to feel loved and cherished is all I crave and want to feel.
Yes! I'm afraid of tomorrow,
I don't want to hear of any more sorrow.
With ever increasing age, one feels time is running out.
How do I set about feeling different,
looking forward and outward?
The sun may be shining outside, even spring is approaching fast.
How can anyone escape this tunnel of no hope
And spring forth once again?
Do I make myself plain?
It might just as well rain,
for no matter how I'm feeling inside.
from you Lord I can't hide!
You know me inside out, faults, warts and all.
Are you the inner voice within me day and night?
I'm thinking this, am I right?
I can only wonder!
But what I seek most at this moment is peace of mind and content.
So please stay with me forever, especially tomorrow,
as I need you in my uncertain mind...
be kind,
and most of all let me find
Peace of mind.

9/3/2008

---

* Written prior to a dreaded hospital visit.

No Sex Tonight

No sex tonight, I have a headache…
That's your plea!
No sex tonight, I'm hungry,
Where's my tea?
How often do we make this the excuse?
Not often your excuse—
Usually it's me.
What shall we do instead?
No use me suggesting an early night in bed,
you might then get the wrong idea
saying something I don't want to hear!
And isn't it quite clear?
I want to relax and read my book,
I don't even want to cook.
That's why you got a sandwich on a plate,
something that I know you hate,
but I couldn't be bothered, mate,
and now it's much too late!.
So once again I'm going to state,
No sex tonight, now I have a head-ache too,
finally—that's my plea!.
I've just had an idea!
Join me, and bring us up a cup of tea!

1/10/2008

Pause and Listen

Do you listen?
Really listen?
Or are you like many people,
butting in before someone can finish?

It's very hard to listen *and* hear,
often it's just fear
that we won't get our point across,
which is a great loss.

It's like a conversation with someone who has a stutter,
you mutter,
and shouldn't do it,
but the temptation is so great,
you just can't wait,
and so you finish off their sentence!.

But do try to pause and listen,
in this fast moving world today,
we can only hope and pray,
that maybe—God—will listen
to us, when we say,
Make our world a better, and a safer place
for another day.

26/9/2008

Road Bullies

We have something new on the road today…
It's maybe called 'overtakingitis'?
For no matter what speed you do,
it's never fast enough,
they cut you up—rough!
And it's tough.

If you dare to complain,
it's just no use,
because they do it again, and again.

So what is their excuse
for manners so gross?
I'm at a loss!

They bully us, it seems,
it's just not fair,
we have a right to be there!.

White vans are especially good at this,
I just sit and hiss
wondering how on earth they miss
colliding with others!

These vans are bullies and so aggressive,
that I'm getting obsessive,
their driving is so bad,
it makes me really mad!

Do they have a right
just because they're white?
I don't think so!

Then again, they are not the only ones,
4 x 4's with nudge bars,
Mercedes and other cars
overtake as well!
So 'what the hell',
if you can't beat them,
join them!
I'm off now to buy something large, maybe
something white,
then I can bully too,
and serve them right!
It'll be a 4 x 4 with nudge bars complete,
then I really can compete!
I'll also get it right
and buy one that's white!

On second thoughts,
I've changed my mind,
for I'm really not that kind.

I think they're really sad
to be driving so bad,
their manners leave much to be desired,
and I get really tired,
but to their level I wont go down,
I'll just amble into town,
go just as slow as I like,
maybe even overtake a bike.

But I really do hate the White Vans!
Those Road Bullies…

17/10/2008

Sixty-Five, Eh?

So you're sixty-five,
You're still alive!
With age you have more memories to look back on
than forward to.
With age, you do more of turning back the page.
With luck, you've learned along the road of life to treasure people,
more than possessions acquired along the way!.
With age, we acquire wisdom, we may pass on our knowledge and wisdom,
But do people listen?
Sometimes, maybe!
But often not,
Why? Because many people just have to learn it seems, by making their own
mistakes.
However, I'm seventy,
So please, listen to me, especially when I say.
Live for today.
Come what may.
And I'll sincerely pray,
That, you'll always live another day.

9/6/2008

Surreal Feelings∞

To truly love someone is so very different to—just chemistry between two
people that ends with really good sex!

With the latter, once the novelty wears off,
there's nothing left! Only

memories of shared moments of such intense pleasure,
feelings that linger well into the years,
even after death! But....

even memories stir up feelings—long since forgotten.
almost unbelievable joyous emotion
not thought possible,
only by one who has experienced it!

But still that is not true love, but...
just a chemistry so strong, that
it can be like a drug—that gives
irresistible craving,
unquenchable,
surreal.

Sometimes in the conscious mind
it's a strange, odd emotion,
to almost find fulfilment with that someone, long gone...

7/10/2008

∞ I wrote this originally for a friend who was bereaved, but it's also there for anyone
to read who's lost their partner.

The Blackout

Last night power was interrupted for just three hours,
one advantage—we talked!
How many others did the same I wonder?

Candlelight can be so romantic, when you choose it,
not so when it's forced upon you.

But way back in the past, in the literally 'dark ages' and
before the invention of electricity, light was only in the form of
Candles and Oil lamps.

So how did the population exist?
But they did of course, because, 'what you never had, you never missed!'
In those primitive times there were larger families.
Purely because there was no TV, no Radio, no Mod. Cons, so to keep warm,
these earlier beings went to bed to keep warm.
And the rest is history—
hence the larger families!

But was it all so bad?
They probably talked much more than this present generation does,
our generation, always rushing here and there seemingly!
Getting nowhere.

But with the passage of time, inventions came along.

Firstly power, I assume, then our modern-day inventions followed,
Radio, TV, Washing Machines, Vacuum Cleaners, Microwaves...

But last night suddenly, out of nowhere, off went the TV,
and we scurried around searching for torches, and matches
to light candles.

And for a short while we were transported back in time.
Was it a good thing, or bad?
Sometimes it's sad, that we don't talk enough,
but would we really want to go back to how our forefathers lived ?
I don't think so,
but just for a short while it makes you think and realise,
how lucky we are.

Or are we?

The Bubble...Oooo...Oooo...

The bubble has burst!
And how it hurts!

A similarity to 'rape'—
Not much hope of escape!

Sitting down to lunch,
And turning on the radio,
You're treated to the latest news
About the 'credit crunch'.

This latest trouble,
This gigantic bubble,
Is a worldwide loss of shares, money, housing and jobs...
We hear of redundancies,
Re-possessions, total loss.
These tragedies are gross.

This literally affects everyone,
There are no exceptions,
Not much hope of escape!
Just like 'RAPE'.

Where will it all end
My friend?

No one knows the answer yet!
It's a 'wait and see' time
Not easy if you're in line
For job loss,
Or any loss!

It's at times like these
We need to believe
That we will get through it all.

It's always darkest before the dawn,
So maybe dawn is closer than we think!
And we're not just on the brink,
But near to the final stage...

19/10/2008

The Closed Door

I'm not a happy bunny—not any more,
I know that for sure,
I'm not a happy bunny!
NO—not any more.

What would change my feelings?
I don't really know,
just a loving hug from someone,
someone close,
a long way it would go!

Just a show of feeling from that someone
would help so much I know, but
if the feeling isn't there,
does it mean that they don't care?
Why can't we just share
Time to talk, and to listen,
not just be a slot in their busy life?

But get to listen to what I say.
Perhaps there'll come a day,
when we *can* talk, come what may!
I really do hope and pray
that later on, perhaps even today,
the phone may ring and I'll hear her voice,
for—that's my choice.

Wouldn't that be nice?

The phone call came,
But—things are still the same,
so I'll just have to play the waiting game.

For whatever it is that's wrong,
I'll be the last to know.
What I want
is to be her confidante.

But that won't happen for sure,
to me—she's always been a closed door.

5/10/2008

The Demise of Monty

We've got a new car
and collected it today.
It has a CD player,
it's colour – a nice shade of grey.

To Monty the Mondeo,
we had to say 'Goodbye'
he failed his MOT last week,
and now is garaged in the sky.

He'd been our good friend in the past,
but nothing will forever last!

We hope that our new car
will be another friend,
and serve as good as Monty did
to the bitter end.

9/10/2008

The Male Species

Why can't men multi-task,
as we women do?

Think about it! I'm not kidding,
it really is true!

Ask a man to do an extra chore,
just one more!

It's a waste of time,
both his and mine.
Because it's something men can't do,
and that's true!

What is so different about their brain?
Or—do they have a brain?

Why don't they use it?
If they don't—they could lose it!

But I'm still trying to work out why
Even if they try
Men can't do more than one task!

4/10/2008

The Third Eye

The third eye sees what our two eyes don't envisage,
It looks way past what is normally visible, and
Takes in a whole different perspective, of an object or person.
Therefore it sees way beyond the obvious, as it looks to the future.

It sees beyond the surface of a person, thus
Stripping the superficial, and
Views the inner being.

Is it the vision of the 'sixth sense'?
Something we do not all of us perceive?

This gift, and it is a gift,
Is a lift, so
If you have it, use it.

The third eye is debateable to some.
Is it a vision?
Is it what is termed 'the mind's eye'?
Something one can visualize internally,
therefore not classed as reality?

Whatever it may be, some of us have it.
A gift from God perhaps,

The Third Eye...

17/8/2008

They Say...

Who are they, who 'say'?
They have plenty to say,
So, what do they say?

They say—'Time and Tide wait for no man.'
They say— 'The Grass is Greener' (but is it?)
They say— 'What goes around, comes around' (does it?)

'Beauty is in the eye of the beholder.'
Spilt some salt? 'Throw some over your shoulder!'

But where do these sayings come from?
Way back in the past, no doubt,

Other sayings—

'Marry in haste, repent at leisure'
'Change the name, but not the letter'
'Change for worse, and not for the better'.

'Ne'er cast a clout,
'Til May is out!'
'When in doubt
 Do now't!'

These people who say—who are they?

They say—'A leopard doesn't change his spots'
'As one door closes, another door opens'
'Rain before seven, shine before eleven...'

'Love and hate are much akin'
'Better to have loved and lost, than never to have loved at all'

'Pride comes before a fall!'

Another saying—

'Would you rather be an old man's darling than a young man's slave?'
                    (Or both?) How true is that?

'Too many cooks spoil the broth'
'What you've never had, you never miss'
                    (A blind person perhaps?}
'A little knowledge is a dangerous thing!'
'A problem shared is a problem halved.'

They Say—
'Life begins at Forty' (It's a long time until Forty!)
'One man's meat is another man's poison'
'Look before you leap'
'There's no such thing as a free lunch' (How true!)

'Absence makes the heart grow fonder'
'Too much absence makes it wonder?'

'A bird in hand is worth two in the bush'
'A wise man learns from other people's mistakes,
        —a fool learns from his own!'

                    They say…

'Blood is thicker than water'
'You can choose your friends, but you're stuck with your relations'
                    (How true is that!).
'Look after the pennies, and the pounds will look after themselves'
'Cleanliness is next to Godliness'
'Red skies at night, shepherd's delight'—whilst….
'Red skies in the morning, shepherd's warning!'

                A few more to come yet…

'Many a good tune played on an old fiddle'
'Many a true word spoken in jest'
'Many hands make light work'
'I wasn't born on a milk float!'… In other words, I'm not that slow!
'You can't teach an old dog new tricks.'

- 'He who shits on the road must expect flies on his return!'
  — a West African Saying!
- 'A farmer makes a plan!'   — a South African Afrikaans saying.
- 'Blessed are the meek, for they shall inherit the earth' (Matt 5:5)
- 'All things work together for good for those that love the Lord '
  — (Romans 8:28)
  (A good friend contributed these four sayings!)

'The quickest way to a Man's heart is through his stomach'
'Anyone can get a man, keeping him is the problem!'
'It's no use being the richest man in the graveyard'
  (Don't strive for earthly riches, in other words!)

'The sights you see when you haven't got a gun...'
  (Maybe just as well for someone!)
'If you play with fire, you'll get your fingers burnt'
'If brains were dynamite, he wouldn't have enough to blow his hat off!'
'Everyone has a right to be ugly, but he abuses the privilege.'

♣

Just a few short sayings...

'An apple a day keeps the doctor away.'
'If the cap fits, wear it!'
'No use crying over spilt milk.'
'Speculate to accumulate.'
'Travel broadens the mind.'
'Listeners seldom hear any good of themselves.'

'While there's life, there's hope!'
'If he had a brain, he'd be dangerous.'
'I experienced ugliness today.' (If someone wasn't very good looking.)
'That fixed his little red wagon!'
  (American? A version of 'Revenge is sweet!')
'I don't give a rats patootie.'
'Money talks and bullshit walks.'
'Still waters run deep.'
'There's no smoke without fire.'

Then there's these Sayings—I think we're nearly there…

'He has pub constipation—he can't pass one.'
'Live each day as if it's your last—one day you'll be right.'
'Not enough room to swing a cat!'
'Every cloud has a silver lining.'
'Sticks and stones may break your bones, but words can never hurt you.'
'He fell from the ugly tree, and hit every branch on the way down.'

(Poor Man!)

'He has a face like a bulldog chewing a wasp!'

(Whereas…)

'She's so ugly, her lipstick curls back into it's tube!'

…and they still keep coming to mind…

'Better the devil you know!'
'Only the good die young.'
'It's not what you know, but who you know.'
'No peace for the wicked!' (Shouldn't be so wicked then…)
'It's better to give than to receive.'
'Some people fall in shit, and come out smelling of roses!'

♣

Well I must draw a line somewhere under all these sayings, as there are so
many it could become never ending! So I'll leave with this one last 'saying':
'

'All's well that ends well!'

2/8/2008

Time...or the lack of it

Time, the one commodity we all lack enough of these days:
We chase time furtively,
hunting it down, just as our ancestors chased food in earlier times.

Whatever we do or say,
when it comes down to it, there is only ever 24 hours in any given day.

Time, search for it until you find it!
Get your priorities right,
find time for work and play,
find time to say
'Hello' to anyone you meet each day;
give yourself time to pray,
but remember, there are only 24 hours in each day,
so come what may,
at the end of each day...

Find time to wind down and relax,
make time to just sit and muse...
make time for a break from work and routine,
a chance to recharge your batteries.

Give time to anyone who needs you to listen,
such a valuable gift, give it if you can,
whether it's your gift to a woman or man!

So many of us multi-task each day,
so, take time out to laugh and play,
leave the unimportant for another day,
please listen to what I say,
for come what may
with luck, there'll be another day.

We all have an allotted time on 'earth'
So give yourself 'me' time. Pamper, relax, wind down, treat yourself,
clear your mind of intruding thoughts,
meditate!
procrastinate!
Yes, procrastinate—if it's not important, leave it until tomorrow.

At the end of each day, leave time to—

Enjoy the serenity to sit and reflect the wonderful gift of silence.
Don't leave things too late,
don't shut the gate,
you can do anything you want,
don't say you can't.

For time never stands still.

27/8/2008

To See or Not to See

I went to the opticians the other week
Because I couldn't see!
'How can I help?' he asked,
Looking straight at me!
'I'm having trouble reading,' I explained.
The words were not as clear as they should be:
We went into a darkened room;
Then he asked, ' What can you see?'
'Not a lot,' I told him.
I'm thinking, 'Is it me?'
After all, I was there for him to put things right!
He took me to a darkened room,
And me with bad eyesight!
After this he did some tests
At the end of which,
With luck, I'll sew a button on,
Or maybe sew a stitch.
So after choosing spectacles,
Which cost an arm and leg,
I couldn't take them home with me.
They don't come off the peg.
So be patient, I tell myself: next week you'll get your glasses.
Maybe it'll open up something new for me, an interest perhaps,
Photography, knitting, painting or reading again, perhaps.
In the meantime I'll have to have a think and wait to see,
Just what interest will eventually appeal to me…

June 2008

Uncertainties

What am I afraid of?
Afraid of the unknown,
I'm afraid of my reactions, and
letting myself down.

I wonder why?
I cannot cry
No matter how I try.

I get depressed, downcast,
but usually recover from it fast,
because I mustn't let it last.

Many things I've suffered before,
they all came knocking at my door,
Lord – I – beg and implore!
Please don't ask of me anymore,
For, I'm not sure,
just how I'll react,
and that's a fact !

To go back and pretend, I'll cope,
when I'm so full of doubt,
and without hope!

I'll have to try,
but why,
when I'm scared to live,
and afraid to die.

My shattered nerves
should be nerves of steel,
but I'm a quivering mess,
no less.

What I need is strength,
of mind!
But where do I find
it?
It's something I cannot buy,
no matter how hard I try.

If only I could turn back the page,
at my age,
there are so many things I've learned from the past,
one is, that things don't last.

I think next time around, selfish I would be,
and think of just you and me,
to put others first,
is one of the worst
mistakes that I've made.

I haven't a clue!
What to do!
Or where to go from here
with my irrational fear.

I'm entombed in this state,
for the time being at any rate.

Regrets, yes, I have regrets,
we all have regrets!
Things I should have done,
does anyone really—have none ?
I can't believe that one,
places to where I should have gone.
but with fear and trepidation I run.

So where do I go from here?
For have no fear,
one year
my destiny will be clear—
please let it be next year!.

Help my uncertain mind decide,
let me no longer hide
my secret thoughts and fears inside.

Let me shine forth,
for all I'm worth
whilst on this earth.

Help my mind know what I really want,
I can do anything if I try,
even if I think I can't.

Uncertainty in the past,
let that be outcast
and please let it happen fast.

No more regrets, and what might have been,
the light I have now seen,
I must say and do as I mean.

No more dithering—be positive—be strong!
Do things right, not wrong,
I can do this if I try,
I won't look back, just forward, from now on—
I've known this all along,
but to put it into practice, that's where I went wrong.
Lord help me—help me to be strong!
Give meaning to my life,
cut out the stress and strife,
one more request, give me belief,
that would be such a relief!

10/9/2008

Wait and See

Whatever happens in this life?
" Wait and see!".
If it's meant to happen, it will,
"Just wait and see!"
Be patient, take your time.
Don't be hasty with decisions,
"Wait and see."
Take your time, go with the flow
and don't say—no!
Say perhaps, maybe,
think positive, not negative,
then, "wait and see."
If you can just "wait and see"
the answer will be found one day
to any problem,
"Just you wait and see!"

1/10/2008

What is the Answer?

We live, we die,
We laugh, we cry,
So at the end, why?
Do we find it hard to say goodbye?

There has to be something else,
Are we reborn in the future, somewhere else?
Just like a plant that in midwinter dies,
Then when spring comes, it will once again arise.

Does this theory ring true in any way?
What do you say?

25/6/2008

Who Are You?

What have I done to you that's made you so hard on the surface?
     A surface that I can't scratch!
Do you have a heart hidden somewhere perhaps?
     I'd really like to know!
Where is your compassion? Do you have any?
For if you have any of these things, why do you keep them hidden?
Can you not feel or show any of these things?
Why not?
You may talk to me, but do you ever listen to me? Or
Are you always somewhere else? For
That's how it appears!
Why won't you let me into your world, that privacy that you keep hidden in
the depth of your mind somewhere?
     Does anyone ever see into it?
What can it be that I have, that maybe you envy?
Whatever it is, it's not worth wanting.
     I envy confidence in others!
     I'm too sensitive for my own good.
     But better that than hard and callous!
What's happened to you, to make you into this unfeeling person you've
become?
If only I could open this closed door into your mind,
Into your subconscious.
Maybe that would give me some answers,
For you have erected an invisible wall, a wall that I cannot penetrate.
Will you ever change?
My heart goes out to you, for one day your conscience will plague you,
     It will invade you so much, that it could destroy your mentality, and
send you to the brink of insanity.
Don't ever look for help from outside, as you've always been so private with
your feelings, letting no one in, so much so that, probably no one will be
brave enough to even try.
May the Lord help you,
As I don't know anyone else who can!

23/5/2008

Young Love

Do you remember when we couldn't bear to say goodnight?
Even though the stars were still shining bright!

The days would come and go,
We loved each other so!

We felt alive only when together,
No matter what the weather.

Our love kept us warm,
Cocooned and free from harm!

Teenage love, that's lasted through the years,
Through laughter, sadness and tears!

I'd do it all again,
Walk with arms around you, in the pouring rain.

If only I could
I surely would!

Wonderful memories, that no one can steal,
But memories that are still—very, very real.

When you're in love, time stands still,
It happened then, and it always will!

1/6/2008

The Start of Something New

There are so many beginnings in life,
Too many to encapsulate!
Where do I start?
How about…
Beginning with the beat of a heart,.
A new life, a newborn baby?
Then maybe
Carry on through life
Where a man takes him a wife.
In today's world, there's no such thing as a job for life.
Sometimes people have to diversify.
Why?
Simply to live—they change course,
A new challenge, begin a new career.
Maybe gain a "Doctorate"—
Another string to their bow.
They learned something new
And so their confidence grew.
Another beginning,
They're winning.
And so it goes on,
Until much later in life, their dream to retire, perhaps to the sea,
Becomes a reality,
Another change of direction…
But on reflection
The beginning of retirement,
Time on their hands,
"Me time"—a great time to begin a new hobby,
Golf perhaps, walking, caravanning, the ideas are endless,
But whatever you choose to do,
Begin today
Don't delay,
Never procrastinate,
Or it could be too late.

Freedom

The engine roared
Giving me a buzz.
This had been my dream
For so long now.
And at long last—it's become a reality.
Fruition!
I'm sitting behind the wheel of my car.
Yes! You've guessed it!
At last after numerous attempts,
I've cracked it,
Torn up the 'L' plates,
I've passed my driving test!
Now I'm going to really learn,
I can go wherever I choose.
No one sitting beside me—telling me, " turn left or right"…
Yes—that's right.
This is my freedom at last,
My new beginning.

Inside Out

This is the moment I've been waiting for.
Counting the days down to.
And now that day has arrived,
I'm scared!
How will I cope with this new beginning—after all these years?
Years cooped up,
The only fresh air being a walk once a day around the courtyard.
But—this time I'll go straight.
The only time I want now,
Is the time on my watch face.
I know I've said this before—and slipped back into old habits.
But I'm getting too old now,
And I've learned that time is precious.
Doing time is a mug's game.
So however hard it will be on the outside,
There's no more going back inside for me.
I've been such a fool, wasting so much of my life.
Whatever is left now, I want to be—free!
Free as the birds!
Free to come and go as I please.
I'll go down on my knees if I have to,
To get some work and money.
I don't want much from life.
I don't want any more strife.
I just want peace and contentment.
I'll pray to the Lord for it, I'll probably need his help,
To stop me succumbing to any more crime.

In just a short time,
Those gates will open and I'll be a free man!
Facing a new beginning.
So help me Lord, I'll need it.

No more sinning for me…

My Way Forward[*]

Today is the first day of the rest of my life,

I've cut the strings.

I'm free—left home—starting out on my own!

Excited, scary, happy.

Today is my dream come true,

I escaped at last from YOU.

The past is just that now—the past!

It's gone, just a memory.

The future, well whatever it holds,

I'm on my own now.

This is my new beginning…

8/11/2008

---

[*] Written about someone leaving home for the first time, e.g. for college, or university.

Part II

Reflections in Prose

Table of Contents: Prose

A Busload of Cheers

When my fiancé and I decided to get married he was stationed at Catterick Camp doing his National Service. Because of this I had to arrange our wedding in just ten days—no easy feat!

By the time Dave had bought my wedding ring and paid for a special marriage licence, he was broke. And so we began married life literally stony broke. It was of course a very quiet wedding, with just two witnesses and a few relations. My one Aunt had travelled down from Yorkshire for the occasion.

We couldn't afford a honeymoon as such, and unbeknown to us my Father had asked my Aunt if we could go back with her to Sowerby Bridge, a small village outside Halifax. We gratefully accepted her offer when she put it to us.

We arrived after a very long train journey, having been delayed at Huddersfield for half an hour while they changed the engine, etc., boarded a taxi that we even had to share in Halifax before eventually arriving at Sowerby Bridge. It was now 2 a.m. in the morning as we got our case out of the taxi and went inside the small cottage.

What was left of the night, we all went off to bed exhausted!

The next morning I got up and went downstairs to get a cup of tea. My Aunt was already up and saucily enquired if we'd slept alright. While she made the tea, I stood looking around at the small front room-come kitchen—when a double-decker bus passed by. To my amazement it was full of workmen, all waving and cheering. I couldn't at this point see why, and thought they were just being friendly. It wasn't until I went back upstairs to our bedroom and on passing a full-length mirror did I realise—that I was only wearing a black nylon nightdress, completely see-through. Oh well, possibly it had made their journey to work a little more interesting.

Her small terraced cottage was on the main road (the conveniences a little further up the road, just near to a bus stop). We were so happy to be married and having a few days together before Dave went off to Germany to serve his time, that these small embarrassing details didn't bother either of us.

We never had a great deal of money all our married life, but once Dave was demobbed, we were just happy being together; after all, money isn't everything. As long as there is love between you, you can get through most things that life throws at you. We certainly did!

Beth Richards. 14/10/2008

A Century, Not Out!

Mary, sitting comfortably in her chair, was wondering what the fuss around her was all about. After all it was just another day to her. She glanced down at her gnarled hands, with her fading eyesight. And with her hearing getting more muffled she sensed people and voices around her, but these days things were not as clear as in years gone by.

Her mind however was as razor sharp and keen as it ever was. From time to time nowadays she drifted away into the far distant past and remembered how she and Harry had met all those years ago and fallen madly in love.

From the moment she had met Harry, she knew she was destined to marry him. Yes, they had their ups and downs like most couples, but they 'never let the sun go down on their wrath'. Sadly they were parted during the war years, but Mary's prayers were answered and Harry came back to her. The Lord had looked after him—many weren't so lucky! Also, they had just the one son, who was a good boy and gave them no serious trouble.

Mary came back to the present and realized that the people behind the muffled voices she'd heard were now doing something to her hair. "Oh, why are they fussing with my hair?" she thought with exasperation. "Why don't they leave me alone?"

A little while later on it appeared they'd gone away and things were calm and peaceful again. Now everything had quietened down Mary's thoughts (as they often did these days), wandered back to her Harry again. He'd been so ill for a long time and suddenly widowhood was thrust upon her. Her son Mark, bless him, took care of everything, as Mary was inconsolable.

Harry had been in her life for so many years and now he was gone forever. Mark, her rock at this time, insisted that she went to live with him and his wife Sarah. This turned out to be one very great mistake, a disaster in fact, as Mary and Sarah had never got on well.

Mary was sad, distraught and inwardly felt afraid. Sarah, on the other hand, much as she tried to make things pleasant for the old lady, felt anger and resentment well up inside her to such an extent that after about eighteen months she confronted Mark one day and gave him an ultimatum: " It's your Mother or me!"

So what was the poor man to do? After all, Sarah was his wife, so it was Mary who'd have to go. And that's how Mary ended up in a care home.

They were very kind to her and really she was happier there in the long run because she now had company, whereas living with Mark and Sarah she was alone for a lot of the time when they went out and left her.

Mary awoke from her little daydream to noise again. There were people coming and going, cards were given to her to open—even one from The Queen! She was given a beautiful bouquet of flowers. (She'd always loved flowers.) Then food was brought in, a cake with many candles on.

At this moment flashbulbs started going off. Apparently it's someone's birthday, Mary thought! With her muffled hearing and dimming eyesight she hadn't realized that she was the special person whose birthday it was.

"You are 100 today, Mary!" they told her, "and it'll be in the Local Paper."
A Century and not out, she thought!

But sadly, just ten days later Mary died—quite peacefully, in her sleep.

April 2008

A Silent Invasion—A UFO, or What!

My name is Jack and I'll always wonder if it was my imagination playing tricks with me. Was it a dream, or something else?

I'll tell you what happened on that fateful day in June, the year 2001.

I awoke to a beautiful early morning sunrise, something I often did, and lay there listening to the 'dawn chorus'—one of the many joys of life, I'd always felt.

I began to plan my day in my mind. I was no longer tied to a schedule, so could please myself entirely what I would do nowadays.

My Wife had passed away some three years ago now, so I only had myself to please. Back in the old days when there was the two of us, it had been so different. We were soul mates, so life had been hard to adjust to, but time eases the pain and one eventually learns to live again.

I'd gotten into a routine that suited me nowadays, so often I'd go down into the village and have a quiet drink with a few acquaintances. That day was no exception, so I decided to do just that.

I normally walked to 'The Crispin' but for some unexplained reason I took the car this time. It was a nice day and, as always, when I go by car I keep to soft drinks.

We sat outside in the pub garden, old Joe, one of my mates, and myself; then later on I decided to go for a drive through the countryside. After all, these days I had nothing to rush home for apart from the task of mowing the grass and I thought, 'Blow it today, the grass can wait!'

So I set off, driving along through leafy country lanes, with a CD playing in the car. Not a care in the world! I'd had a large roll with my drink back at 'The Crispin' so I wouldn't be needing food just yet. I rose up higher and higher into the Peak District, the most wonderful scenery imaginable, and when I reached a very remote desolate spot I stopped the car, adjusted the seat, and in the warmth of the sun I closed my eyes and drifted off to sleep.

I awoke some while later to find it was getting somewhat chilly. On looking around I decided to look for a pub and grab a bite to eat, for I was beginning to feel hunger pains.

After driving for a short while I came across a pub, 'The Cat and Fiddle.' I got talking to a few regulars who told me that it was one of the highest pubs in England, and actually straddled several different counties.

I enjoyed my meal and it was whilst driving back home that this strange happening took place. In the past I'd read in the newspapers about strange happenings in this part of the Peak District, but thought it too far fetched to be true. Now I'm not too sure.

There are few lights in this part of the countryside, so I was driving along with the car lights on of course, when suddenly through the trees a shape appeared to be hovering. I could see it as if it were a spherical glowing shape, which was descending silently into a field.

I turned off the engine of my car and sat in silence, mesmerized, my breathing now quite shallow. I don't remember what I was feeling—fear, excitement, perhaps, but certainly I was in a somewhat confused state.

This craft with its lights glowing eerily in the blackness of the night, and the silence all around, was awesome to say the least. I sat there for what seemed an eternity before anything happened. Nothing specific happened until then, apart from the fact that the night sky was radiant with a glow of light.

The whole scene was quite eerie. Trees at night always appear somewhat grim and stark. I shivered—I don't know why, or whether I was just cold, but for some reason I was transfixed by the whole scenario, and also curious.

Suddenly a door resembling a chute opened and these creatures emerged. What are they, I wondered? I was intrigued to know, but had no way of finding out. All I could do was to sit and watch and by now it was way into the night. Time seemed to stand still.

As suddenly as this craft had appeared from out of the night sky, the creatures disappeared back inside, then without a sound it glided upwards without any trace of ever having been there!

I turned on the engine once again in my car and made my way back home. After a night like that, then tossing and turning, I began to wonder the next morning whether I'd dreamt it all—that is, until I saw something in the newspapers about a strange happening in the 'Peaks'.

Was that what I had witnessed, I wonder?

What would you think if you were me?

Divine Intervention?

I'm Jill, and I would like you to read this short story about a very strange incident and see what you think.

My late Father was the eldest of a family of ten children. They had large families in days gone by, for obvious reasons. His name was Bob (short for Robert of course).

Dad was a farmer originally, and came from the North of England. But circumstances forced him South in the 1930's, where he met my Mother and they married just three months later.

For forty years the only contact he had with his family was by letter and Christmas cards, as all those years ago, way back, people didn't have telephones; also, Dad was a very bad traveller.

I grew up and married my Husband Ray. We had two children, Shirley and David. They were my parents' only grandchildren as I was an only child. I think this was mainly because I was born just before the outbreak of the Second World War!

They do say that a woman marries someone like her Father and incidentally Ray too was a bad traveller, just like my Father! Ray couldn't travel by coach, but once he learned to drive, he improved considerably. So we began going on holiday with a caravan that we towed with our car.

On one of our holidays we chose to visit some of Dad's relations up North, at least the ones who were still alive by then. We enjoyed some really good times with my Aunt and Uncle, who still had a farm. On a Saturday night we would all go into the cosy sitting room and sit chatting with a log fire blazing in the grate, our dog laid out on the rug. The room had quite low-beamed ceilings, small windows and the walls were about two feet thick. Uncle would sit back in his chair smoking his pipe while the rest of us sat chatting. How I envied them what was my dream farm cottage. Ray and I would love to retire somewhere like that one day.

With some careful planning we organized a surprise visit of my Cousins, Aunt and Uncle, and children, etc., a total number of fifteen in all for one Sunday that summer.

They all piled into a mini-bus which they'd hired for the trip. They knew Dad's address of course; all we had to do was finalise where and what time to meet them.

With a great deal of trepidation and excitement Ray and I waited around the corner of my Dad's bungalow. Now the moment had come, I was feeling a little nervous as this would be the first time the two brothers had met in forty years. (As it turned out it was the last.) But I needn't have worried; once the initial shock and emotion passed the two brothers went off up the garden together, Dad showing his brother with pride his beautiful flowers and vegetables, and his greenhouse. Dad's garden had always been his pride and joy. I took a lovely photo of the two of them together. While they were gone, my Mother and Aunt talked together indoors. After all, this was the very first time that they'd met. More cups of tea and finally Dad's family were off to see the sights of London on their way back home.

I was so pleased that I had been instrumental in arranging their meeting, for there was a ten-year age gap between the brothers, and sadly they didn't meet again, as my Father passed away a few years later.

Being his only daughter, Ray and I had to make all the funeral arrangements, choose hymns, etc., to be played. Both my Father and Mother had been chapel-going people, and so I remembered one of Dad's favourite hymns was, 'In Heavenly Love Abiding'—which I chose to be played at his funeral.

During the few years after my Father died, his brother who'd always suffered with a heart problem, had quite a bad stroke. He did survive that stroke, but for his six remaining years, he never regained his speech. Ray and I visited him and my Aunt on many occasions whenever we were on holiday up North. The strange thing was that he always seemed to know me, and would just say the one word—'Hello.' He always knew what I said to him, and kissed me goodbye.

One day Uncle Donald fell, and that was the end, for he didn't regain consciousness and soon afterwards suffered a massive heart attack.

Although it was a long way to travel for a funeral, we did go for my Aunt and Cousins' sake, to support them. It was a very long day for us, one I'll never forget as I'd never seen anything like it before; you see, the whole village turned out to say goodbye to my Uncle. Even the village shop closed out of respect. The cars stretched from my Uncle's farm to the Village Church where he was to be buried, which was about one mile away.

We all got into our cars and followed the hearse. There were twenty-two cars in the procession, and by the time the last one left the farm, the first one was arriving at the Church. Just outside the Church gate the vicar awaited us and called out for the relations to line up. I was Uncle Donald's only niece in the long line of the procession.

The small Church was packed. We were ushered into the pews and into the seats that were reserved for us. Before long the service began.

I was totally filled with emotion by now, *but* when I noticed the hymn that was to be sung, I nudged Ray as I could not believe the coincidence. Yes, you guessed, it was 'In Heavenly Love Abiding'!

Apparently one of my cousins had chosen the hymn for her Father, and because it was a Methodist hymn, to be sung in a Church of England Service, they had to apply for special permission to use it.

The service over, we walked slowly down to the grave and stood in groups, silently as one does on these occasions, some tearful and comforting each other. I stood with Ray quietly thinking while the coffin was lowered into the grave. My thoughts were of what a wonderful, peaceful and serene place to be at rest, the hills around so beautiful—a pity that those lying there couldn't see the glorious scenery that we standing there could see. But maybe they could—how do we know for sure that they can't?

The irony about all this is the fact that no one from the family came to my late Father's funeral—after all, they did live some 150 miles away—so they had no idea that this particular hymn chosen for my Uncle's funeral had also been played for my Father. After all, had it been 'Abide With Me' that is so often chosen for funerals, it wouldn't have been so strange!

Was it, then, just a million to one chance? A coincidence? Or maybe some divine intervention from the Lord?

I'll never know the answer, but what would you say?

11/7/2008

Forbidden Fruit

Why do we always want something just a bit out of reach, something we know we shouldn't have? That's what happened in the Garden of Eden, and what started it all. There are many kinds of love, but the one I'm going to illustrate in this story falls into the same category of forbidden fruit!

My name is Anne, and I learned the hard way that we don't choose who we fall in love with, or I certainly wouldn't have chosen Ernest. To me—well, he was the 'love of my life' at that moment. But sadly for me—he was a Married Man.

Many girls do exactly the same as I did, to their cost.

My experience of love (or was it lust?) for this Married Man began at work, in the office, and as for many other girls and women, it ended in tears!

To begin with, I was very young and naïve at the time, having already worked in several offices. Although I was only 16 years old, I'd found it difficult to settle down—until I met Ernest!

Ernest was my boss. He singled me out and at first I found it very exciting. Also, I was flattered, I suppose, that he was attracted to me, because he had a wife and two children.

It didn't occur to me that anyone would get hurt—that's how stupid I was in the beginning.

He was old enough to be my Father, so *he* at least should have known better. But I suppose it was just a bit of fun to him—having a 16-year-old to flirt with, for that's what it was in the very beginning.

For the first time I began to look forward to work. It meant seeing Ernest, but if for any reason he wasn't there that day, I felt disappointed—and should have seen the warning signs. But by now it was too late.

I dreamed of Ernest taking me in his arms and telling me he loved me. (Which, incidentally, he never did—tell me he loved me, I mean!)

However, when we were working together in the office at times, he was teaching me various aspects of work and would sit just about as close as possible, touching me if he thought that no one would notice. Whether they did notice, I don't know—but gradually one thing led to another. Then, one lunchtime, we were on our own and it was then that he kissed me for the first time. I melted into his arms, my breathing erratic and my stomach doing a somersault. It felt good—and I wanted some more.

This was the first time I'd ever felt these kinds of emotions. It became like a drug—the more kisses we shared, also fondling—the deeper I got carried away. I lived for these stolen moments of passion.

However, being his bit on the side was a very lonely game. After all, Ernest had the best of both worlds. (These married men always do!) He had me, and he had his wife and children to go home to. I had nothing much, just a few stolen moments of ecstasy!

One night I was leaving the office and walking towards my home when Ernest drew up alongside me in his car. I didn't need much persuasion to get in and we went for a drive and parked in a lonely lane. He certainly knew how to get around the parts of my body to excite and thrill my whole being. He was very careful not to go just that bit too far, but what I was feeling inside escalated me totally out of this world. Had he gone just that bit further I certainly would have reached a climatic end, a heaven on earth sensation.

Why do we always want the apple that's out of reach? The unattainable? Because of the thrill and excitement, I suppose.

On another night Ernest drove us into the heart of the nearby Parkland, into the privacy of the secluded trees. It was wonderful lying there in his arms, the world of work non existent—to me anyway.

We never went further than him fondling my breasts and caressing me in such a way that if he'd wanted, he could have taken me. But he didn't!

This clandestine little affair of secret meetings went on for about eighteen months, with me falling head over heels in love with this man. But what could I expect from it? Nothing at all at the end of the day. For these types of men very rarely leave their wives and families for their little bit of extra-marital pleasure.

During this time I spent some very lonely weekends and holidays.

Our meetings did end unexpectedly, caused by the return of one of the office staff from military service—Douglas, who incidentally happened to be Ernest's brother-in-law. One of my female colleagues thought the sun shone out of Douglas—he could do no wrong in her eyes.

As for myself—well, Douglas and I never hit it off. Whether he suspected something about Ernest and myself I don't know—but the short outcome of it all was the fact that after a few months of trying to get on with him without much success, I applied for another job. I handed in my notice as soon as my application was successful.

My last day at work was uneventful, until I began my walk home that night. I'd said my goodbyes and departed, and while walking along, Ernest met me in his car. We talked; he really thought that my leaving was because of female jealousy. However, when I told him the truth about the situation he realized that it was impossible for me to stay.

We kissed goodbye—passionately—and that concluded our little affair. I walked away totally bereft and broken hearted.

The first week in my new job I was totally miserable. This time there was only myself and the boss working together in the office, but it was okay as my new boss was old enough to be my Grandfather! In time he turned out to be a generous boss, kind and very considerate.

One day, after I'd been working for him for some time, he confided in me that I got the job as I was the only applicant who had fallen for him. (In a big way!). The joke was that on the day of the interview, the cleaners had just polished the corridor floor and in my 5" heels I had made a grand entrance by sliding the length of the corridor on my bum! So my new boss had a sense of humour!

For a long time after I'd left Ernest's employment I often walked my dog, either past his house, or near to where the office was in the hope that I'd catch sight of him. I very seldom did! It took me a long time to get over him.

I really thought I'd loved him. During this period in my life I would play sad romantic songs in my room, which often ended in me crying more tears—fool that I was.

Gradually I began to move on and because of this trauma (which it certainly was to me at the time), I began to notice other young men who worked nearby, and one of them had apparently noticed me—that new girl working next door; after all, I was still only barely nineteen.

Much later on this admirer became my Husband, and so something good and positive came out of my total misery for loving a married man. And this time I didn't have to plan secret trysts—we could be seen out together and show the world our love for each other without shame.

However, many women, both young and old, fall into the trap of loving a married man. You could warn them of the consequences and folly of this—but it would make no difference whatsoever, because (at the end of the day) you don't choose who you fall in love with.

And so you see, my story really did begin way back in the Garden of Eden—with Adam & Eve and the apple, the forbidden fruit that proved such a temptation.

My Posh Friend

My friend who shall remain nameless rang me up last night, once again at a crossroads in her life. We've all been there at some time, so I knew just what she was going through.

We first met at school some 60 years ago and became good friends. She is one of a family of five girls, unlike myself, an only child. But she's the nearest I've got to having a sister!

We've confided in each other so many times over the years, telling each other our secrets. She's even told me things she was unable to tell her sisters. So that shows how great and deep our friendship is!

My name is Patsy, and I'll tell you my story now.

But to go back to the beginning when we met at school—we were drawn together by the fact that I was being bullied and 'Posh', as I'll nickname her, was teased somewhat because she spoke better than most of the other school kids. So we teamed up together and we're still great friends, although through circumstances we now live the length of the country apart.

We had some good laughs, Posh and I. One night we'd played a game of tennis at the Manor House, near to where Posh lived. On the way home we had to jump over a ditch to get to the lane and—guess what? I fell in, of course, consequently getting soaked! So Posh lent me some of her clothes, and when I arrived home my Mother was not amused!

We left school at the same time—there is just one month's difference in our ages—and started work. Meeting often on a Monday night, we'd get all dressed up and queue for half price tickets at the local theatre. We really thought we were 'with it'!

I don't think either of us had many serious boyfriends. I do remember my first kiss, which wasn't very exciting. Once I met my future husband, though, that was it! I knew straightaway he was the one.

Before we were married Posh and I went on holiday together to Spain. On the beach the holidaymakers lay in the sun. Some wore very skimpy bikinis, not leaving much to the imagination, whilst others were topless. After some discussion Posh and I decided to go topless! We'd agreed, 'I will if you do'—and so there we lay eventually with our 'bare bits' (tits!) like ice cream cones pointing skywards. Suddenly—plop!—an overenthusiastic seagull dropped the inevitable straight onto my cones! Of all the thousands on the beach, it had to choose yours truly on whom to deliver its parcel! We did both laugh nevertheless as Posh helped me to clean up.

Posh got married a year before me, when she married Jimmie who'd just finished his apprenticeship. He was due to do his National Service, but he failed his medical and was exempt on the grounds of bad hearing.

The next year I married John, who passed A1. We decided to marry and get the marriage allowance. We intended to marry as soon as he was demobbed anyway, so we just brought things forward. Our wedding night and our first attempt at full intercourse, the condom broke! (Luckily I didn't get pregnant. Until then we'd never gone all the way.)

I was so envious of Posh who didn't have to endure the two years of heartache and separation that John and I went through. But I needn't have envied my friend, as she was widowed at a very young age. I'll come to that later.

During John's time away from me (he was posted to Germany), Posh had her first baby, a daughter. When I saw her baby lying there in her Moses basket, so beautiful and Posh so proud, I was pleased for my friend, but at the same time it made me feel wistful—for I knew it was going to be a long wait until John and I could start a family. After all, we hadn't even got a home of our own; I was still living at home with my parents until John was demobbed.

This was my one cherished wish—I'd always wanted a house, a husband and baby, and knew I'd never be fulfilled until I'd got them. So far I was married to John, but had a long way to go before my dream would be complete.

John and I wrote to each other every day while he was away, unless he was out on a scheme somewhere; then I might get two or three letters at once after a gap of a few days. Sometimes on a moonlight night I would gaze out of my bedroom window up at the moon and stars, and it was a small comfort to know that wherever we were in the world, it's the same old moon that shone on us both! That moon was my shining light to sanity. We both counted the days and crossed them off the calendar towards John's demob day. I really couldn't wait to start our lives together, as those two years were a slice out of our lives.

We'd got married with next to nothing moneywise, and were hard up for a great deal of our married life. If happiness had depended on wealth, we would have had a very unhappy marriage. But so long as we had each other, we didn't want anything else.

During the next few years Posh had her second baby. And eventually after a lot of trying, I had our son.

Our children used to play together whenever Posh and I met up for a cuppa and a chat in the afternoons. This went on until Jimmie was in line for being made redundant. Posh persuaded him to move to a really large house on the outskirts of town to run a B&B, which turned out to be very successful. During this period we lost touch, just sending each other Christmas and Birthday cards.

I never knew the reason, but after a few years they moved to a bungalow, but sadly six months later Jimmie died of a Brain Haemorrhage. Posh was widowed at the young age of just 50.

It was some years later that we met one day, and she was on the arm of another man. I didn't recognise her! Such a lot of water had gone under the bridge, but when she spoke, it was her voice I recognised—the same 'posh' voice that hadn't changed.

It was very good to see her again, but I wasn't sure about her new partner at all. We often got together again socially and I tolerated him because of our friendship.

We both moved house. John and I retired up north, while Posh and Luke moved south. All this happened in the space of a few months. Twice they came and stayed with us, and we stayed with them a couple of times down south. But there was something about Luke that I didn't trust. He was so different from Jimmie, her late husband, who had been far more educated and gentlemanly. Luke was the complete opposite, noisy and very excitable. But even so we remained friends, keeping in touch by telephone.

It was just the other night that she phoned me with such an extraordinary tale—a dilemma if ever there was one, and it took her two hours to relate it to me.

My friend was very upset, that much I could tell by her quivering voice; but once she controlled her emotions, what enfolded was totally bizarre!

It appeared that Luke was at the centre of this drama—and how! Once Posh got down to explaining the nitty-gritty of it all, I was gobsmacked, for although I never really liked him or trusted him, I wasn't ready for what he'd done.

It had started once before, apparently, at the beginning of their relationship, and Posh had never told me then—she'd brushed it under the carpet—and they'd agreed to start again.

But this time he'd really overstepped the mark. I'd always suspected him of being a 'ladies man' and a bit of a charmer, even a con artist, but his barefaced cheek took the biscuit.

Posh had suspected he was up to his old tricks as far back as two years, but didn't want to face up to the truth. He would be gone for much longer than necessary just to do a simple errand of shopping. His plausible excuses were wearing a bit thin, but I think by now my friend had misplaced her spectacles (those rose coloured ones) as she began to see through him!

For years, Posh and one of her sisters, Ruby, had always been very close, and often spent the weekends together. Posh and Luke, Ruby and Mark, they all got on well together. A bit too well apparently!

She broke down again, and then composed herself before going on.

It was on one of their weekend stays with Posh and Luke, that the penny suddenly dropped. They had a drink, the four of them at a local pub, as they often did, when Posh noticed that Luke and Ruby were missing and she was left talking with Mark. She said," I suddenly felt uneasy" and that her heart felt cold and heavy as lead. She told me very quietly, " I suddenly *knew*, this isn't right, and wondered, what's going on here?

"I said to Mark, 'Where are the others? Come on, let's go and find them.' So we set off together towards the woodland area at the rear of the pub. No one usually wandered up there, but instinct drew me towards it.

"Wending our way through the trees, I summoned Mark to listen! I could faintly hear giggling. So we stealthily ventured towards where it appeared to be coming from.

"We stumbled across a glade in an opening, and at that moment my heart froze. I was staggered, for there was my sister and my partner oblivious to the world as they lay together, completely naked--making love! (Lady Chatterley's Lover came to mind!) She was gasping with sheer delight; they were far too engrossed with each other to notice the presence of Mark and myself. And for the moment we were too dumfounded to do or say anything.

"They were certainly caught in the act! Luke suddenly turned around, and I screamed at him, 'Talk yourself out of that one!' as I fled, quickly followed by Mark on my heels, heading back towards the pub.

"It was bad enough," she said, "finding out that Luke had been unfaithful, but with my *own sister!* How *could* he? Or even, how could she do this to *me?*"

The irony is that it had been Ruby all those years ago at the beginning of their relationship as well. By this time she was quietly crying and there I was, the length of the country away from my dearest friend and all I can do was listen! I couldn't even give her a hug! I couldn't even tell her that everything would be alright, for in my heart this time I didn't think it would be.

I am so sorry that my dislike for Luke, my feelings of mistrust for him, were correct right from the start, and didn't turn out to be just a silly mistake.

I don't know if Posh will forgive him again as they've been together now for well over twenty years, but I know that I never can. What he's done to my friend is despicable beyond words or comprehension.

30/8/2008

My Story

Here I was at the age of forty speeding up the M1 to meet an Aunt and Uncle for the first time. Little did I know that this would alter my life completely.

When we eventually arrived in a Derbyshire village the scenery took my breath away. The more I went back year after year it never failed to do just that, time and time again. Until I had seen Derbyshire (my late Father's birthplace), we had always taken our holidays in Devon and Cornwall, but after that first visit I was totally smitten. We had a touring caravan, so every weekend possible we would hitch up and trek up the M1, the Derbyshire destination always the same—I couldn't get enough of it!

During the course of about twenty years I also got to know my five cousins and their families. My Aunt and Uncle always made us welcome. My Aunt became like a Mother to me—she is still alive at the age of ninety-two! Twice during these years my husband was made redundant (they say lightning doesn't strike twice in the same place, but for us it did).

The first time we thought about moving North we wondered about running a Bed and Breakfast, but it wasn't meant to be—we couldn't sell our house so that dream didn't materialize. When it happened again six years later my husband tried one or two jobs; we were both getting older and by this time my daughter had presented us with a grandson we both adored.

My husband hated what he was doing job-wise, as he was no longer working in his trade. He tried very hard to persuade me to move again. In all it took him about three years to persuade me to take the plunge and put our house on the market. The big problem was the idea of leaving my daughter and grandson—I really felt torn two ways!

As luck would have it, we put the house on the market and fell in love with a bungalow outside Chesterfield. Once my mind was made up and despite the upheaval involved, we were set to move in September of that year. It had taken us eight months to complete the move, but from the moment we moved in, we knew we'd done the right thing.

Now our retirement had begun, what else were we going to do? I had begun writing poetry years before in my thirties and now, for once in my life, I had some "me time"! So apart from writing poetry I took up Oil Painting— something I'd always wanted to do.

Before long I had my first book published, which was exciting. My poetic thinking didn't stop, so I had another book of poetry published which included a short bedtime story.

I wrote a third book of poetry, then decided it was time to write a novel, which was published earlier this year.

My next step? Who knows?

Has my life changed? And how!

I would like to add that although it's nearly a year since my novel *Journey Towards A Dream* was published, I still continue to write poetry which seems to come naturally and straight from my heart. Recently this led to the little volume *Worlds Apart*, a joint effort between myself and fellow poet, Charles Muller; indeed, we worked very well together.

I still paint in Oils and get totally absorbed when working on a painting, and this I find totally relaxing.

For me these are purely hobbies and are not about making money, but about giving other people pleasure in reading my poetry and perhaps one day hanging one of my paintings in their home, thus giving them something pleasurable to look at.

For at the end of the day, whatever we achieve in life, whatever we may be worth, "In the end we all will be, Just A Memory…"

Beth Richards, Author/Painter

My Trouble and Strife

As the husband of a wife who's got us into so much debt in the past with credit cards, etc., on account of her foolhardy spending sprees, the latest incident involving Police and possibly a Court Appearance has really driven me to the brink of insanity. I really don't know if I can cope with any more. The latest incident happened the other night—when I returned home from work as usual.

My name is Paul, and my wife is Sheila, who is a checkout assistant at the local supermarket.

When I arrived home that night it was unusually quiet. We have two sons, the eldest who is out to work and the younger one who's at school.

I was thinking to myself, "Where the hell is Sheila?" She should have been home hours ago. So I began ringing around—my Mum, Sheila's Mum, her friends, all to no avail!

I was now beginning to panic inwardly and trying to keep calm for the sake of the boys. By now, it was pitch dark, and the shrill of the phone sent a bloodcurdling shiver right through me. But it was just a call from my Mum to see if there was any news. When I told her I'd drawn a complete blank she said, "Well Son, we'll have to ring around the hospitals and see if she's been in some kind of accident."

So—well into the night now, there we were ringing the hospitals with the mystery getting deeper, because it just appeared as though Sheila had vanished into oblivion, with no trace.

Desperate by now I began ringing around the Police Stations, and finally to my utter disbelief and dismay I was told that Sheila had been arrested that day and was being held overnight in a Police Cell.

Now Sheila had done some daft, crazy things in the past, but never got herself arrested!

They advised me to try and get some sleep, as it was now 3 a.m. But how the hell was I expected to sleep with everything going through my confused mind? I had been in debt for twenty-five years with a bank loan, taken out because of Sheila's love of spending on the credit card, money we didn't have. But it was like a drug to her; she had to have things regardless of how much debt she piled up. But this time I'd no idea what trouble she was in, or even if I could bail her out of this mess. I punched the settee with clenched fists in consternation.

For the rest of the night I prowled around like an animal looking for food, making coffee to stem the sleep deprivation of the night. At daybreak I just wished I could either go back to bed and sleep, or wake up and find that all this was just a nightmare.
Sadly, though, it was for real. So I went through the motions of having a quick wash, giving a shave a miss in my anxiety to get Sheila out of that Police Cell as soon as possible. Looking at my unshaven reflection in the bathroom mirror I thought—"My God, I've aged ten years overnight!"

Sheila's Mum arrived to take Sam to school while I went off to the Police Station. How I got there—I don't know, mainly because I knew the route so well. Just my luck, it happened to be a foggy start to the day, so after being up all night, with my eyes feeling like they've been in a clash with sandpaper, I was peering through the gloom. Cars with headlights on didn't help much either, but at last I was through the traffic, parked my car and entered the door of the Police Station.

After explaining who I'd come for, I sat and waited. Eventually Sheila emerged with a woman Police Officer. She looked white-faced and drained. I didn't know what to say or do, mainly because she looked so vulnerable. So I said nothing! She looked at me for some sign of reaction, but all I could manage was to steer her towards the door—and into our car.

We drove home in complete silence!

Once we were home I prayed to myself—"Whatever she's done this time, Lord, please help me, help both of us, because we're gonna need it!"

After the strained journey home where neither of us had spoken, I faced Sheila. Her eyes, I could tell, were full of glistening unshed tears, her face set in a fearful expression.

All the tensions of the previous night suddenly exploded from within me, and whereas I'm normally a quiet man, I shouted at her: "What the bloody hell have you done this time!"

We went at it hammer and tongs then; such a lot of hatred spewed forth, both accusing each other of things that I'd thought were long forgotten. This went on until we were both utterly spent!

When we'd both eventually calmed down enough to speak to each other in a more civilized manner, she told me what it was that had led to her arrest.

Apparently the store had been watching her for some considerable time, as they had been suspicious she was acting fraudulently. They had to be 100% sure before taking any action, and had set a trap.

She proceeded to tell me what happened. She was on her till as usual—*but*, the customer whose goods she was scanning was a friend. Now Sheila knows the company rules do not allow you to serve anyone who's either a friend, or family in case you are tempted to put anything through without it registering. I was so exasperated at this point as she knew she was doing wrong! She said she knew it was wrong, but took a chance.

What she omitted to tell me there and then was the fact she'd been doing it for a long time. Why, I asked? Sheila replied that in the first instance she'd done it for Thelma as she knew she was down on her luck and had kids to feed, so she said, "I felt sorry for her."

Then she admitted that it seemed an easy thing to do and they then hatched up a scheme where she gave Thelma a list of goods that she knew we needed ourselves. Thelma would get her shopping at the same time, and they sorted out the goods when they met up later.

"Oh Sheila, you bloody fool!" I yelled. "Didn't it occur to you that you could be caught?"

"Well, it seemed so easy, Paul," she sniffed. "It didn't enter my head, until I saw the Police and Manager approaching my till. Then I knew I'd been rumbled. I pleaded with them to just give me a caution, but they wouldn't listen, as I'd been watched on camera without me realizing it!

"So I was arrested, handcuffed, and taken off in the Police Car, and now I've been sacked, have no job, no references with not much hope of finding another job—certainly no one will employ me in any way connected with money involved!"

She then broke down in uncontrollable sobs. But I refused to be swayed by all this display of emotion and walked out of the door with her pleading me to forgive her.

I walked off down the steep hill that led to my Mother's house. I knew she was as worried as myself during the night when we couldn't find out where Sheila had disappeared to.

Somehow I had to tell Mum what crime Sheila had committed—but I didn't know how to, mainly because my poor Mother was ill herself and not in a fit state to hear about Sheila's latest stupidity. Mum knew what a life I'd had with her and her debt problems (she'd even bailed us out with money in the past) but I didn't think money would get Sheila out of this mess!

As I walked down the road, there were cars passing by, people too, maybe even some of them I knew—but I was in such a turmoil of emotions that it was like I was isolated in an air bubble.

I reached Mum's house at last. It was not that far from where I lived (but it seemed an eternity since I left Sheila), my mind so crowded with the thoughts of what Sheila had done, and what I'd do, *and* most of all how to tell my Mother; also, what her reaction would be.

She must have seen me approaching. The door opened and with an incredulous look on her face, she gasped: "Whatever is it, son? Lord, you look as though you've seen a ghost or something!"

She guided me through to her sitting room and got me a small glass from the cabinet, pouring a small whisky out. She placed it into my shaking hands and I gulped it down in one go.

Haltingly I related to Mum what I knew so far and what Sheila had got herself involved with. I could see she was aghast. Like myself, she was wondering how Sheila could have been so bloody naïve and stupid.

However, Mum kept repeating that Sheila hadn't stolen any money as such, only been caught in the act of passing goods through the till to her friend. But I went on to point out, "She's guilty of fraud by deliberately giving away company goods worth Lord knows how much, as she's been doing it for a long time. Into the bargain we've been eating and living on stolen food, too. Can't you see, Mum, she might just as well have been taking money out of the till."

"What will happen to her, Paul?" she asked me.

"I don't know, Mum. I'm at the end of my tether—after all the trouble she's got us into during our married life, I just don't know what to do. Even her own Mother, who won't normally hear a word against her, is disgusted. I feel so ashamed as it'll probably get into the local paper eventually."

I certainly didn't want to tell Mum all this, as she was under a lot of stress herself with health problems, and could do without me adding my worries.

Before I left her she asked me what I'm going to do, and I answered wearily, "I really don't know"—because at that moment, and indeed at this moment, I have no idea of the outcome. Unless a miracle occurs, Sheila will probably end up in Court, with maybe even a custodial sentence. They might be lenient with her because of Sam, our youngest.

Whatever happens is in the lap of the Gods, but what I'm finding hard to endure is the fact that—I can't seem to live without her, and now I feel that—I can't live with her.

Before we even find out Sheila's fate, the last straw came when I was informed my firm was making me redundant. Quite clearly, my luck is out at the moment.

My Troubled World

In the very beginning I had absolutely no idea how my one and only son, Guy, would one day turn my whole world upside down.

He was such an angelic baby, a delightful child and I absolutely adored him. Later I would ask myself many times over, how did I produce such a human being and then, for him, one day to father my one and only grandchild?

Guy was a clever boy; he went through his teenage years without the usual tantrums that so many of my friends endured. They thought I was so lucky, but much later on I would gladly have changed places with some of them.

Guy went off to University to study Chemistry and Biology. Although I missed him, we kept in close contact and he always appeared to be having a good time at University with his friends. He made friends easily, but not many girlfriends, and it didn't really occur to me that this was odd in any way. It should have sent out warning signals to me, and looking back I can see, now, how naïve I was about this. Apparently at University there were two girls that Guy was friendly with. It turned out that they were lesbians!

All those years ago that kind of thing was kept under wraps and not generally made public, only to close and immediate friends. And Guy was their friend.

To Sybil and Joyce their unusual relationship was only marred by one thing, the fact that they couldn't have a child—the one thing they both desperately longed for.

Unbeknown to me, Guy had no interest in women sexually, but Sybil and Joyce wanted a child so badly that they approached Guy to help them in their desire for a child. IVF Treatment was in its infancy and quite expensive, but my lovely son agreed to be the donor for their child, providing that they go abroad to live eventually after they'd finished at University.

On one of his vacations Guy broke the news to me that he'd realized he'd never be a father himself by taking a wife, as he'd known for a very long time that he was gay!

I then felt so stupid that I'd never guessed this for myself, and that he'd had to tell me. How naïve I'd been!

It was Sybil who wanted to give birth to their child, so it was she who'd had the fertility treatment. Luckily, it worked first time, as it was so expensive. The agreement between the three of them was that Guy would go out to New Zealand at regular intervals. It was what he wanted and he also helps financially with the boy's upbringing.

So now I have a grandson, my one and only, in these very strange circumstances.
Curiosity got the better of me when Mark was getting on for 3-years-old, as all I'd ever seen of him were photos. So I asked Guy if I could go with him on one of his visits. I was very apprehensive about going, but curiosity propelled me forward, and I went.

I can't truthfully say that I enjoyed the trip. I've been now, and of course Mark had absolutely no idea who the elderly lady was!

I'm ashamed to say that I have no feelings for the child whatsoever. I know he's the only grandchild I'm ever likely to have and I feel sad because of that knowledge, but he might just as well have been a neighbour's child to me. As far as I'm concerned he lives on the other side of the world and I've no desire to ever see him again.

Guy certainly knew how to turn my world upside down, but it's not his fault. It's just the way he was made, I guess.

4/5/2008

Surreal, Bizarre – would you Adam and Eve it?

I've never really been one to believe in the afterlife or supernatural stuff—ghosts or anything like that—*but* something happened recently that's really made me question my views! I'll tell you about it—maybe it'll make you wonder, as it has me! My name is Pam. I'm a widow living on my own since my husband of forty years passed away a couple of years ago, and much as I've searched my mind I can find no logical explanation for a strange, surreal happening.

When he was alive my 'Tom' was quite a heavy smoker. Something I've never taken up, but I can still visualize him sitting comfortably and lighting up. His party trick to amuse any visitors, especially children, would be to make three smoke rings appear.

They reckon that someone bereaved goes through many different stages of grief, one of them being anger! I went through anger myself, thinking, "Why did you go and leave me all alone?" I was so angry with Tom at that moment in my life.

However, as I intimated, a very strange thing happened earlier today.

To go back to this morning, the newspaper arrived and I tugged it out of the letterbox, glancing at the front page with all the usual doom and gloom. But the first page I always turn to is the Horoscopes. I know it's probably a load of tosh, but nonetheless I love it, and old habits die hard. Apparently someone admires me from afar, so I think—"Oh, that's nice, I wonder who that can be at my age!" But beggars can't be choosy, of course!

Later the doorbell rang and on opening it, I found—just the milkman collecting his money.

Later after breakfast I'd just made myself a drink when the phone rang. On answering it, there was no one there! This often happens, so I took no notice.

♣

It's a Saturday afternoon but I'm not interested in Grandstand, racing or football, as Tom used to be. So I make myself comfortable, put another couple of logs on the fire and do a little thinking.

Scruffy, my little cat, makes herself cosy, curling up as she does near to the fire.

The winter afternoons look gloomy outside, but with the logs crackling, a couple of hours later I light one of the table lamps.

"Oh drat!" I think to myself, "That damned phone again!"—just as I'm nicely settled in my chair. Because the phone is in the hall, I get up to answer it.

A man's voice enquires: "Hello, is that Pam?"

"Yes, it is, but I'm sorry, I don't recognise your voice!" I reply. "Who is it?"

"I'm a friend of Tom's," he explains. "It's Charlie."

Well, at this point I'm mystified as I don't remember Tom ever mentioning a friend called Charlie!

"I'm sorry," he says, "I've been so long getting in touch, but it's nice talking to you Pam. Is Tom there, I wonder, as I haven't seen him in ages? And for some reason today I thought, 'I really must give old Tom a bell and see how things are!'"   I let him finish and then quietly told him that Tom passed away a couple of years ago.

There was a silence at the other end of the line before Charlie spoke again. "Oh Pam, I'd no idea! I wish now I'd rung him before."

After Charlie's initial shock we chatted on for a little while. Apparently they'd met many years ago whilst serving together in the forces and had lost touch. Now it occurred to me why I'd not heard Tom mention Charlie, for he never spoke much about his time away.

It turned out that Charlie only lived approximately. 70 miles from my home, a distance travelled quite easily in a day. So before putting the phone down, he tentatively broached the possibility of calling to meet me quite soon.

I didn't really know quite what to say in answer, as he was a complete stranger to me; so I asked for his phone number and promised I'd contact him when it was convenient. Also, it gave me time to think!

I gently replaced the phone on it's cradle, and when glancing at my watch I realised I'd been talking longer than I thought.

But—Charlie did have a lovely mellow voice, one that I could easily listen to for hours. A little voice inside me was calling out: "Be cautious!"—*yet* for some reason I felt I'd like to meet Charlie and get to know him better. Also, I looked forward to the prospect of being able to talk to him in depth about Tom!

I did find that soon after Tom died people would avoid talking about him. Maybe they did this in case it upset me too much.

But I couldn't help thinking now that it would be nice talking about Tom, preferably with Charlie—a complete stranger.

"Oh well," I thought, "I have Charlie's phone number, so I'll mull it over and then perhaps give him a ring in a week or two. After all, it won't hurt just talking on the phone." I was still arguing, you see, with that persistent little voice nagging in my head!

I entered my sitting room door and gasped incredulously! The smell was quite distinctive—no mistaking what it was, *but*—how? It was the smell of Benson & Hedges cigarettes that Tom had always smoked.

At first I thought it was pure imagination and probably something to do with the dying log in the grate. But then I noticed in the corner near the chair where Tom often sat, there were three smoke rings!

Suddenly scruffy took one look at me and jumped up—her fur bristling and with her tail stiff as a poker, she fled out of the room as though the devil himself were chasing her.

I sat down quickly as my legs folded like jelly from under me. I watched for some while; it seemed an eternity before the smoke rings eventually disappeared. I shivered, and then put some more logs on the dying embers.

As I said at the beginning of this story, I've never believed in these kinds of things.
But after today I don't know any more…

In time I did phone Charlie and we built up quite a rapport before eventually meeting.

So my horoscope on that fateful day could have been correct about someone admiring me from afar. Or did Tom arrange for Charlie to come into my life and look after me?

I'll probably never know the answer to that—but I must admit that it's lovely having someone in my life again after those years on my own since Tom died.

It's a very lonely life being a widow. I wasn't looking for love again at my age, just companionship!

That Was the Year, That Was...

My name is Sally. The year was 2001, and so many good things were on the menu for this particular year, but sadly things don't always go the way we would like. Harry, my husband of nearly 50 years, wanted all the things that I did. Nothing different there, as we'd always been soul mates. But this particular year of special events didn't exactly come up to our expectations. I'm an optimist, however, so it takes quite a lot to dampen my spirits. "There's always another year," I think to myself, "with a bit of help from the Lord above."

♣

To begin with, I'd been working really hard for at least the last three years to write a novel, and now in the early spring of 2001, I had achieved my ambition, for my 'dream' was at last published.

It had all begun with an idea dating back to three years ago, and everything we do in life begins with an idea. Whether we persevere with it, is up to us! I'm of a determined nature, so I got on and wrote my novel, but to begin with I'd asked my publisher what he thought of the first chapter, and I trusted his judgement when he replied, "If you write it, I'll publish it." So there it was, in print early in 2001.

It'll probably never be a bestseller, but to me the important thing was that I'd achieved what I'd set out to do and that was what mattered. They say that everyone has at least one novel in them and now I've written mine, so I'm happy with that.

The same year, 2001, my husband and I reached our 50th. Wedding Anniversary, another achievement in today's world! Sadly, things didn't go to plan on this—what should have been a momentous occasion. We had asked that there wouldn't be a lot of fuss, a party, etc., as we are not really much given to parties. But that didn't mean we wanted it killed stone dead! A lovely bouquet of flowers and some cards, perhaps, would do nicely. We had some lovely cards and good wishes from our friends, but as for family—that was a complete letdown!

We'd planned a short holiday break on a complex site with a David Bellamy award, so set off full of hope. On arriving in the heat of the midday sun, we ambled across to the reception office and to our dismay, were asked whether we'd booked direct, or through a travel agent?

Though confused by this, and as it was lunchtime, we had a stroll around before returning to the reception office. The welcome from the staff was somewhat cool, compared with the heat outside. We became a little suspicious and apprehensive, wondering if there had been a double booking!

After what seemed an eternity, we were at last taken down to our accommodation, where another surprise awaited us. To our knowledge we'd booked a log cabin. Although the outside was timber clad, on entering, the inside was clearly based on a caravan layout. This was something we've not entertained in years as they don't have the stability and comfort of a genuine log cabin. Certainly, on the basis of this alone, we were disappointed. We'd only booked this particular holiday to try and have a short break—just the two of us—because everything we'd tried to suggest doing with our only daughter wasn't convenient for one reason or another.

We looked around this glorified caravan and I decided to have a lie down, to try and relax. My rest was shattered by the shock I got in the bedroom— when I looked up above the bed, the light fitting was not only broken, but bare wires were hanging down. I called to Harry to come and look, and he, being a retired electrical engineer, was aghast! "Thank goodness there aren't any children in here," he remarked.

That night we had a violent storm. I wasn't surprised as it had been so hot during the day. After having a poor night's sleep and finding no coffee table to even put cups on, the accommodation being so poorly equipped, we tried sitting out on the veranda the next morning. But the smell was so awful outside! We opted for a walk around the complex. It turned out that the sewerage and waste disposal point was the cause of the horrible smell, and there were flies by the millions!

We went back and ate a sandwich, then thought we'll try our luck at finding the nearest village. One needed a compass for that, as it appeared we were in the middle of nowhere, with very limited signs to anywhere!

Eventually we tracked down the elusive village with just a couple of shops after a detour around country lanes and no one in sight to ask directions. We bought a couple of the most expensive commodities (bare essentials really) and returned to the site. (An open prison, really, as one had a key to lift a bar to gain entry either out of, or into, this so called site.)

After the stormy night it was once again baking hot, so we went for a lie down, and being deprived of so much sleep the previous night, we both drifted off. When we awoke I made up some salad for dinner and Harry asked, "Where would you like to go tomorrow, dear?" I meekly replied, "Home!" And that's exactly what we did. The whole break, which should have been so wonderful by the description in the brochure, was a complete nightmare. No way could I get back into the holiday spirit and enjoy it. It had been a complete let down.

What else could possibly go wrong this year, I wondered?

Time was now moving rapidly forward towards my 70th birthday. Again I requested that I didn't want anything much, really, as by the time one gets to this age, if you've been lucky, you have most of what you want. But as it was one of the big birthdays, my friends sent me some lovely cards and messages of goodwill. The first card that I received was from my daughter. It didn't please me much as it was one of those funny cards, which, incidentally, she knows I don't care for, and in due course I told her so. So she replaced it with another lovely card. But why do I have to tell her? She's 45 years old, for heaven's sake, so she's not a child and should know me by now.

Harry and I decided it was to be a day trip somewhere in the car for my birthday. So off we went to a local beauty spot and parked the car. Even that proved to be a problem. Harry put the coins in—and no ticket! And he couldn't get the money back either. Other couples were apparently having the same problem. Harry began to get cross, and by then it had started to rain. We decided to make our way back towards home and called in at the supermarket on the way. Harry went off for the trolley and of all things the coin got stuck and wouldn't budge! His temper was really frayed by now and he wouldn't even go to the service desk to get that sorted. Even I was feeling dejected by now. The rain was, by now, pouring down, and so I decided, enough was enough, so we went home.

I'd had my present from Harry, but he'd always bought me a surprise one, and this year it was a garden gnome. (I do love my garden). As I was unwrapping it, it just fell out of my now, arthritic hands, landing on the floor minus his head! Harry and I just looked at each other and burst into helpless laughter. If I hadn't laughed, I'd surely have cried! But someone had it in for me on my 70th birthday—the birthday from hell, that neither Harry nor I will forget in a hurry!

I think in the future years to come (that's if I'm lucky enough to survive many more), I'll do the safe thing and forget all about birthdays. I'll remain at 70 now for however many more I clock up. After all, they say that "every day is a bonus after three-score years and ten!"

One good thing to come out of the year 2001 was my novel being published and in print. As for the rest of the year, well, it proves one thing—"Never expect too much; you can plan what you like, but it's all in the lap of the Gods as to whether it turns out good or bad!"

So, 2001—that was *the* Year, that was!

June 2008

The Holiday

It was early on a misty morning that Louise stood by the window watching the   blackbird. It was busily searching for its breakfast on the dew-sparkled grass; perhaps it had babies to feed, seeing it was that time of year!

There were two of them strutting around, one keeping guard or acting as a lookout for the ginger tom that frequently visits our garden. Oh! All of a sudden she's got lucky, cocking her head and listening so intently, then jabbing at the ground before pulling out a nice fat worm. Love's labour, I thought, as I pictured her nest hidden carefully from view, her babies somewhere eagerly awaiting their food, little beaks upturned at the ready. How delightful nature is!

All young creatures are the same, relying completely on their mother from birth, to both feed and nourish them. Isn't it a pity, I think to myself, that we all have to grow up and lose some of the trust we have as infants?

These days I often wish I could have someone to comfort me in times of uncertainty, but with age these luxuries are rare.

Why am I standing here today, a little heavy of heart? Why? Because tomorrow my daughter and family are off on their annual holiday abroad. And although these days I don't see much of them visually, it's so much easier to contact them when they are in the same country.

The world these days is in so much turmoil that I wonder at times if there will be another tomorrow? Or will some tragedy, an earthquake or plane disaster strike, and that million to one chance will rob me of my little family, thus killing—my world!

My daughter's name is Sue. Roger is my son-in-law and they have Damien, who is now nearly six years old. But they are the only family I have that I care about, except for Matthew, my husband.

In my mind for the next two weeks I'll be imagining where they are, and what they are doing, and with a bit of luck, I'll receive some text messages from time to time. But for those two very long weeks for me, I'll be living their holiday within my own imagination.

Matthew knows only too well that I'll have anxious moments, just hoping and praying that they'll arrive safely and enjoy their holiday time. I know that it's probably selfish of me to want the time to pass quickly, but just like that little blackbird that's been feeding her young chicks, I still care for Sue who is still my baby and always will be to me, however old she is.

I'm beginning to shiver now as I've been standing here for so long. Even the sun is peeping cautiously through. One of the trees throws a shadow across the luscious green, dew-soaked lawn and in its shadow the 'ginger tom' stealthily approaches, but he's too late now. The blackbirds have long gone and I think I'll go back to bed for a little while longer.

The day eventually passes, very slowly for me. I knew that it would. I went through all the normal motions, trying not to let Matt see inside my fuddled brain, but he knows me too well, and that I'm putting on a first-class act, which in no way fools him!

That night we go to bed. It's now 2 a.m. and I'm wide-awake, of course, as it's time for the impending departure. The next two weeks, whatever I do, I'll be trying hard not to—but Sue, Roger and Damien will be in my thoughts.

Everything is always worse in the middle of the night, but dawn is now breaking, Matt is still fast asleep, and I have been wandering around the house, which is eerily silent—except for Matt's gentle breathing. Time drags on, but inwardly I cannot shut down my mind.

At least now it's daylight I can keep myself busy. Before that it's those dreadful few hours when the whole world appears to be sleeping, and only I am awake. That is the worst time—when my mind goes into overdrive!

After a very early text message from Sue, I go through the motions of the day, the usual mundane chores, etc., but a little voice in my head keeps nagging at me until I could scream out loud for it to stop! But it goes on relentlessly, as I try my hardest to just carry on and ignore it.

The daylight is now turning into dusk, the sun sinks gradually down in the west, and I'm now sitting outside in the gloom, with the last drink of the day in my hand. The birds, like myself, are now quietly winding down ready for some longed for sleep, and in the stillness I am aware as I sit quietly, that I'm not alone. The ginger tom cautiously emerges from behind some bushes and I am treated to such an amazing display as I sit with baited breath.

If only I'd got my camera, I could have taken some amazing pictures. At first I wondered what the ginger tom was staring at with such a confused, baffled expression. It was merely a—frog!—that was springing around; he'd obviously been under some rockery plants and stones and thought it was safe to emerge!

The ginger tom's expression had to be seen to be believed. Any movement on my part would have spoilt the show, so I sat in rigid silence. The frog was oblivious to the cat and was thoroughly enjoying his little evening excursion around our lawn. This went on for several minutes. I sat intrigued, the light now getting dimmer and it was beginning to feel chilly.

All of a sudden the ginger tom advanced on the frog, which then hopped straight back into the rockery, and, in so doing, ended the show. Oh well, I sighed to myself, it's getting chilly now, so off to bed again. But how such a trivial event could give one entertainment like that—wonderful!

Oh well, only another 14 days to go before Sue's back in England.

However, out in Portugal, Sue, Roger and Damien were enjoying their holiday. Before they went they'd studied and made lists of all the places of interest to visit, so time was being enjoyed to the full.

Just a text message each day was all that Sue thought was necessary to her parents; after all, we're on holiday, she thought.

With Damien only six years old, they realized quite soon that he's happiest on the beach with his bucket and spade, and with the help of Roger, building sandcastles.

But they all got more out of this than expected, as quite often they were treated to a daily performance just off the shore—by dolphins. They are such exquisite creatures, so enjoyable and entertaining to watch.

The accident happened approximately halfway through the holiday. Damien was playing happily when all of a sudden he screamed out in pain. He was playing in the sand barefoot, of course, and had trodden on a piece of broken glass bottle, carelessly left by someone.

Roger sprang into action, scooped the child up in his arms, blood gushing from his little foot. Sue quickly grabbed a towel to wrap his foot in and that was an abrupt end to the day on the beach. With help from onlookers they managed to locate the Hospital, and spent what seemed an eternity before Damien was cleaned up and they could get back to their holiday site.

Scared as both Sue and Roger had been as a result of the accident, they didn't want to worry Damien's Nanna and Granddad, so messages were kept very short when Sue did text. This, however, didn't fool anyone!

Mum, Louise—back home in England—was somewhat suspicious. Indeed, she always seemed to have a sixth sense about things.

But still, Sue didn't want to worry her, as there wasn't anything she could do, and after all it wasn't a serious injury—so both Roger and Sue thought it better to say nothing. Sue's thoughts were, "What the eye doesn't see, the heart can't grieve over!"

But back in England Louise was eagerly looking forward to her text messages (which she noticed were getting shorter) and counting the days to when Sue would be home again. It was always the same—the first week was the worst; once that was over Louise began counting down the days. She knew it was selfish, but it was her only way of coping.

It was just as well that Sue hadn't mentioned Damien's accident, for Louise was a born worrier—something her daughter knew only too well.

During the days that followed, it was the highlight of Louise's day when the text message arrived; however short they were, they gave her peace of mind.

During the second week Louise was crossing off the days on her calendar, happy in the thought that "this time next week, they'll be home again."

Meanwhile in Portugal, Sue, and Roger were secretly wishing their holiday could last forever. "If only we could win a lot of money," Sue said, "we could stay here and start a new life! Oh well, dream on!" Apart from Damien's little accident it had been a brilliant holiday, but all good things come to an end. Then it's back to reality!

The last few days of the holiday passed without incident and now it was nearly time for the return journey. They packed that evening, ready for departure in the early hours of the morning.

Back in England Louise was awake very early (nothing unusual in that!), being the morning she knew Sue and family would be leaving Portugal to fly back home.

At the break of day Louise is once again standing by the window, gazing out into the garden watching five young blackbirds busily hunting around for their breakfast worms. Mother bird has probably stopped gathering their food for them now, she surmises, as birds tend to tip their young out of the nest to fend for themselves at an early age. "It makes me wonder why us humans don't do the same," she reflects. "Certainly it would make sense in my case, especially where Sue is concerned." The beautiful early sunrise has now broken into a bright, sunny blue sky with just a few white fluffy clouds. It's good to be alive on a morning like this, thinks Louise.

Later that day Sue and family return home to a few minor problems. She phones Louise to let her know they are back.

The moral of this short story is, "There are two sides to every coin!" Sue has had a well-deserved holiday and enjoyed her fortnight of freedom from the stresses and strains of everyday life. On the other hand Louise knows that maybe she's selfish in feeling happy now that she knows the family are safely back home.

One small secret I'll now admit to, right at the end of this short story, is this—that I am Louise and I know exactly how it feels when one's daughter is abroad. There is absolutely nothing I can do about it for sure, as next year will probably be the same again. But until then I'll have peace of mind!

When Sue phoned she did tell me about Damien's accident and the reason she'd said nothing at the time, and deep down I know that she is right.

I am just a born worrier!

The 'L' Driver

During breakfast one morning I had an idea—nothing unusual, given that my star sign is 'Leo'—a go-getter, or so I've been told!

At the time I'd just turned thirty. My children were comfortably settled into school life, so I had a little "me time" on my hands—just what I needed to precipitate my latest idea into fruition.

At this point the local newspaper crashed through the letterbox. I picked it up and went straight to the adverts section. There I found what I was looking for—a local Driving Instructor. Later on that day I'd give him a ring, I thought as I got dressed.

And that's how it all began—from my initial idea, which, of course, was to learn to drive.

My name is Emma and now I'll tell you why I had this urge to drive a car. It was an urge my Husband Fred was not too happy about to begin with, but he'd learned over the years that I was not to be easily fobbed off once I'd made my mind up.

Later that day I rang up Thomas and we fixed a date and time for my first lesson, the following Tuesday morning at 11 a.m. We agreed on that time to avoid the morning rush hour because at this stage all I knew about a car was, where to put the petrol in. So I was a complete novice.

My car drew up outside with me now feeling some trepidation and wondering where on earth I'd got this ridiculous idea from? I nervously closed the front door, proceeded towards this alien vehicle, and saying a quick prayer, got into the car.

As this was my first lesson, Thomas drove us to a nearby lay-by and talked me through the basics, beginning with the three pedals—the accelerator, the brake and the clutch pedal. We then changed over seats, I made the necessary adjustments to the mirror etc., and it was time to set off.

After stalling the engine, then finding that this car appeared to run on different petrol to that of our car (petrol Fred jokingly called 'Kangaroo' petrol), I very slowly moved forward towards the open road.

This was what I'd been waiting for—*but* I'd never realised how much there was to driving! Being in the car with Fred for so many years, I never realised the intricacies of driving, for he made it all look so easy. But that's always the way with anything—the expert always gives the impression that it's easy.

At the end of my first lesson Thomas remarked that because of my age, it might take longer before I was ready to take a test. So I booked more lessons and went inside, determined now more than ever to get that piece of paper, the one that gave me a licence to drive.

That night Fred asked me how I'd got on and I sweetly replied, "Fine!"—and thought to myself, "I'll show him! Anything you can do, I can do better!"

The first few lessons were a bit like—swings and roundabouts (I'd never realised that you were expected to make it, sit up and beg!) with one of my main problems being corners. I either approached them too fast, or too slow, whereas—reversing and three point turns were "a piece of cake". Thomas remarked after one of these lessons, "It's a pity you can't reverse up to the corners!"—but determination spurred me on.

Then I encountered my first setback! Thomas had to go into hospital for a hernia operation. (I do hope that my driving hadn't accelerated it!) He suggested that as a good friend of his was willing to teach his pupils until he was recovered enough to resume work, I might like to give it a go with him? Rather than lose time I discussed it with Fred that night and suggested that we put 'L' plates on our car, then drive into the nearby countryside to see whether he thought it worth me carrying on?

This we did, and with a little apprehension we set off together in our car the following weekend, having deposited the kids with a good neighbour for an hour. (That poor neighbour—I hoped they'd be on their best behaviour.)

Now this of course was the very first time I'd been at the wheel of a car without dual control, but considering the fact that Fred had been against me learning from the start, I pulled away on a different car (none of that Kangaroo petrol nonsense now) on a road that wasn't flat and drove quite smoothly, changing up and down through the gears with confidence (at least on the surface)! After a few miles I slowed down, pulled up and shut off the engine.

What do you think I asked? And to my surprise and relief he responded with, "Yes, carry on, you're better than I thought you'd be."

Well, I'd won Fred round, but it still wasn't going to be an easy ride, not by any means as I was shortly to find out. But then nothing in life is worth having if it's not worth fighting for.

The next week I began my lessons with Charles, Thomas's friend. I was a trifle apprehensive but I needn't have been for Charles was the perfect gentleman, both his teaching method and mannerism so different from that of Thomas.

Whereas Thomas appeared abrupt and not very patient at times, Charles encouraged his pupils, which certainly brought out the best in me. His techniques were altogether different. He taught me how to reverse park— something not all instructors teach, for he said, "What's the use of going shopping if you can't park the car?" Very sound advice!

At the end of a month, however, Thomas was well enough to work again, but by now I was happier driving with Charles, and told him so. It was agreed that I would carry on learning with Charles.

I'd never mentioned it to Fred, but sometimes whilst driving with Thomas he would be a little suggestive and I didn't like it; he even went as far as resting a hand fleetingly on my leg on one occasion, and then apologising profusely. Charles, on the other hand, was the perfect gentleman.

It was because Charles was so different I was really beginning to enjoy my driving lessons now, *but* just then—I developed mumps.

I had to abandon my lessons for a short period. However, I was still determined to continue and used this time to really read and digest the Highway Code.

It was on one such morning when I was sitting quietly reading and memorizing details, that I noticed—the cat! Being a trifle cross that it wouldn't move, even with my tapping on the window, he just appeared to be staring at me defiantly, and so I stared back. Suddenly a small grey furry creature scurried along across the lawn. Intrigued, I watched. As if from nowhere another cat was stealthily creeping along on his belly, stalking the mouse. Now these two cats, who belong to a neighbour, are identical 'ginger toms' and so anyone passing by who'd maybe had a skin-full the previous night might have thought they were seeing double. Eventually the poor creature, 'the mouse', which was doomed anyway, was killed by the cat after it tortured it and played with it first. In the past I've often wondered if there was a notice somewhere in my garden displaying a sign: 'Public animal convenience'—as those two cats persistently used my garden for their business requirements! But maybe I shouldn't discourage them too much, or I may acquire some small grey furry lodgers.

It wasn't too long before I was back behind the wheel with Charles instructing me again. By now he reckoned I was ready to apply for a driving test, which he was pretty confident I'd pass first time. Pity I didn't feel quite so sure!

Anyway by the time my appointment came through I was more optimistic about my chances, and on the day itself, much to my surprise—I was feeling somewhat calm.

I was taking my test at Chertsey, a few miles from where I lived, so I wasn't 100% familiar with the area, although most of my lessons had been mainly over there.

It took approximately three-quarters of an hour to drive to the test centre, a little warm up practice. We arrived and my examiner for the test shook my hand and enquired in a somewhat sarcastic tone, "if the car was mine?" Of course, I answered NO, because it was my instructor's car I was using. I didn't exactly warm to him at that point. However, we proceeded with my test and were approximately half way round the course, having done the usual three-point turn (which turned out to be a five-point turn, as the lanes in Chertsey are very narrow), I did my reversing around the corner, and all was going well. No problem with the Emergency Stop.

The point where I'd apparently failed was going around a bend that was unfamiliar to me, as he'd taken me on a different route entirely to those I knew and had practised on. At this point I did the unforgivable by driving straight into someone's driveway. I knew not to panic (as they mention, if you make a mistake, to get out of it safely and you still may not fail); and so I calmly corrected my position, pulled out onto the road and drove back to the test centre.

Charles was so amazed that I'd not passed, but the examiner said I should "know the difference between a road and driveway". The test, apart from that, had been perfect.

Charles was the perfect gentleman yet again whilst driving us back home. This was the difference between his attitude and what Thomas's would have been—they were 'Worlds Apart'. No recriminations whatsoever from Charles!

I applied straight away for a cancellation and took my second test with just one two-hour lesson between, and the next time I passed.

But failing the first time had dented my confidence and I was really nervous on the day, so much so, that we'd gone round the course and were heading up the very narrow, densely parked High Street when I had to wait for the traffic lights to change. During this short time (which seemed an age to me), my left knee was vibrating up and down because I was so uptight; but I never lost control of the clutch pedal, not for a glimmer of a second. I know the examiner noticed as I saw him glance down. I reckon he must have thought, "If she can keep control like that, she's okay to be let loose on the roads"—because when we got back to the test centre, he handed me my pass—my ticket to freedom.

All this in just four months, including the time lost for the mumps!

My reason for wanting to drive in the first place was because Fred was bringing home a van from work—and so our car remained in the garage from one weekend until the next, unless we went out during an evening. Also, Fred and I had endured some rough holidays in the past and I thought it would help me so much if I knew that I could get us home in any emergency, should one arise!

Now I'd got my licence I thought, "Why did I make such a fuss about all that?"—as, like everything in life, once you know how to do something, it's easy.

A few years later we were on holiday down in Devon with the kids and a friend when something funny happened. (Something I was embarrassed about at the time.) Fred took the kids to the beach, while my friend and I went shopping in Kingsbridge. Now if you know Kingsbridge High Street, you'll also know that it's very steep. Unfortunately there was a great deal of traffic that day as it was market day, so about halfway up we had to stop;

when the traffic moved I proceeded as I thought to follow, but the car slipped backwards with me quickly applying the handbrake. Twice I did this and was now beginning to get a trifle flustered. To my dismay a forbidding looking Policeman began to approach the car. I really thought I was in for a telling off, but felt so foolish when he said in a very sarcastic voice, "If you put your car in gear, madam, it will go." My friend suggested wisely, "I think it best not to mention that little incident to Fred—we'll keep it our little secret.."

Many, many years later I did tell Fred what happened in Kingsbridge High Street, long after the death of my friend.

That is my story of what learning to drive is all about, but if you wish to learn for whatever reason, then do give it a go—and I wish you well.......

What a Life!

Throughout my life I've done some regrettable things, but the worst was when I got married for the second time, after being divorced many years before—when my children were young. The unforgivable part of this was—because I did it in secret, without any of my four children being present!

My name by the way is Dawn, and my husband's name is Dan, but what I did, looking back, was really so unforgivable that even I have no excuse for it.

Looking back now on my life I think it reflects a kind of shock tactic that I enjoyed, being the centre of attraction and seeing how people reacted to it. But we only have one stab at life, so no use looking back with regrets. What's done, is done, and can't be undone!

Way back to the years when I got divorced, it was practically unheard of to be divorced. I remember shock waves rippled through my family at the time. But to be quite honest, I enjoyed the part I played in my scandal and I loved the outrageous attention I'd created.

At that time my children were aged twelve, ten, and seven. Although my parents were quite Victorian in their outlook, they took us all into their home. This couldn't have been easy, because in those days they cared deeply about 'what the neighbours would say'!

I settled into a life of domesticity, with some part time jobs for a while, until I became bored with that. After all, although I was a divorcee, in my mind that meant I was a single woman again!

It was then that I began going out dancing, having a drink, etc., and I met someone called Phil. I told myself that I deserved some happiness and pleasure. He was a charmer though, and I fell for his charm in a big way. Much to my downfall!

And so at the age of 40 I had a son—out of wedlock! All those years ago to have an illegitimate child was a disgrace and so once again I'd done the unforgivable, and in doing so had caused a few raised eyebrows. But even that didn't worry me too much. I thrived on this kind of thing.

I loved Phil, Tom's father, very much, but he wouldn't marry me, and because of my circumstances Tom was brought up by my sister—who adored him.

My parents both died during the next few years, so to keep myself afloat financially I took in a lodger. I was forced to do this really because by this time my other children were now grown up with their own lives and families.

Dan had been my lodger for four years and we'd become close during this time, so it was no surprise when he eventually asked me to marry him one night.. I agreed to his proposal, also to keeping it a secret until we were man and wife. Another large mistake!

At our wedding ceremony there were just two witnesses, who were family members that we'd sworn to secrecy from the start.

Now, how do I tell my four children that I've become a Mrs again, and that Dan is now my husband?

In the end I took the cowardly way out, writing to each of them identical letters—then I sat back and waited for the uproar!

My eldest son never did forgive me, and I can't say that I really blame him after all the things I've done in my life!

The others were a little more understanding. But everyone makes some mistakes in their lives; it just seems that on looking back, I've made a career out of it.

Even now—looking back, there isn't much I'd change. Compared with some people I've probably led quite a sensational life!

But who wants to be bored to death?

Not me—no way!.

July 2008

Where Did I Go Wrong?

I really should have seen this coming, but being the naïve and trusting woman I am, I didn't. I'd had my suspicions for a very long time—but really didn't believe they could be right.

My name is Wendy and after twenty-eight years of marriage I'm feeling so devastated that things are now so bad between myself and Richard, my husband.

To go back to the beginning, which was approx. two or three years ago, I began to suspect something was wrong when Richard gave me implausible excuses for his behaviour, e.g. working late occasionally, and dinner with a few colleagues from work the night before we were due to go on holiday to Cornwall. On that occasion he came home at around midnight, knowing that we were planning to leave at the ungodly hour of 3 a.m. to avoid the traffic.

But one of the cheekiest things was playing badminton most weeks with a *female* partner! Often his mobile phone would be switched off when I tried to contact him.

How could I have been so blind? But blind I was, and now I'm paying for it dearly.

Richard has now asked me for a divorce—but I can't give up that easily, because to me marriage is a lifetime commitment. We'd made our vows all those years ago—'until death us do part.' So I'm very reluctant to agree to a divorce, although his asking for one proves that he's probably been unfaithful. In other words, he's committed adultery!

Both Richard and I sat down and agreed to live apart for a while, a cooling off period, and then see how we felt.

During this period I did a lot of thinking. I spent a lot of time with my two horses in our stables. And strange as it may sound, while I'm down there working and grooming them, I talk to them. They are good listeners!

After three months of us being apart we agreed to meet, and I persuaded Richard to come back home. We needed some impartial help to sort out our differences, so Richard agreed to seek the help of a Marriage Guidance Counsellor. We both went together for these sessions.

I suppose that the stress of all this had affected me more than I'd realized, because I began to have panic attacks, which were quite scary. They became so bad and were occurring more and more frequently, so in desperation I sought the help of an expert in this field.

This again, changed my life completely!

I had gotten so low in self-esteem, that I also booked myself in at the local Gym, as I felt that I needed it.

During my sessions with the expert in stress management and panic attacks, I became more and more conscious of my feeling towards Paul, who was helping me on a one-to-one basis.. It arose in conversation one day that he was a millionaire and he made it very clear that he was just as attracted to me as I was to him.

Paul, it seemed, wanted us to become lovers, but while I was still married to Richard I was not going to have an affair. It went against my beliefs!

Knowing all this, Paul promised to buy a large house in the country, with room for my two horses—if I left Richard. Like a fool (which I must have been on looking back), I agreed.

Paul bought the house as promised and moved in some really lovely furniture, all in readiness for us to move in together. I was so happy!

But two months on and there is still no sign of this happening!

Why is it that I seem to attract the kind of men who invariably let me down, as all Paul is now doing is inventing excuses for not coming to live in the house with me?

I'm now wondering if Paul is GAY!

Thank goodness there are no children involved in this dreadful mess.

But, looking back with hindsight (which is always easy), I regret so much the decisions and course of action I've taken!

Amy's Wish

A Short Bedtime Story

Once there was a fairy called "Twinkle" who lived in the mind of a little girl called Amy. No one else could see Twinkle, but to Amy she was very, very real. They would have some very long talks together, sometimes in the garden when Amy was sitting on her swing and sometimes she would be there with Amy at night when she was all tucked up in bed, warm and snug.

Amy was a very quiet little girl and she didn't have many friends, only one or two, and even they didn't know anything about Amy's fairy friend Twinkle.

After Amy had gone to sleep one night she had a dream. Twinkle came to see her and told her to go down into the bottom of her garden where she could meet some of her fairy friends. In the morning when Amy woke up she remembered her dream of the previous night and she didn't say anything to anyone and later on that day she went down into the garden as Twinkle had told her—and what a surprise she had when she got there! She rubbed her eyes because she was so excited at what she saw.

Amy was only a little girl and she knew that nobody would ever believe her! They really wouldn't, so she knew there and then it was her secret forever, just as Twinkle was her secret fairy friend.

After a few moments of standing quietly and watching, Twinkle noticed her and drew her into the glade where there were more fairies dancing.

It was all so exciting and it was right here in her own garden!

By this time the sun was shining and the fairies and Twinkle were shimmering in the sunlight. Amy was nearly afraid to breathe in case they all disappeared. As well as all the fairies, who were all in pretty pink filmy clothes, there were dragon flies swooping around in the sunlight, rabbits hopping around pretty toadstools, squirrels running along the branches of the trees, and birds singing and flying around—all this and much more! It was really unbelievable for a little four-year-old girl.

Twinkle came over to Amy, and to Amy it was just like another fairytale dream. Twinkle was so pretty in her pink dress that was shimmering in the rays of the sunlight. For a long time they talked and gradually the morning, which had started misty, grew brighter. Before long the dew on the grass dried in the sunshine. Amy hadn't realised how the time had gone. She had been so entranced with the happenings of the day that she had forgotten all about time. To the little girl it was another world, but it was beginning to get dusk and the sun was going down and she was feeling both tired and hungry.

Twinkle noticed Amy was tired and suggested she went back into the garden, out of the glade because, as well as Amy being tired, all the animals had gone into their hideaways in the ground and were asleep and all was now quiet and the day's happenings had ended. Suddenly Amy thought no one would ever believe her if she told them her story of Twinkle and everything she'd seen in the glade at the bottom of the garden! But Twinkle promised to visit Amy very soon, so Amy went to sleep that night very happy and waiting for her friend to come to her again one day soon.

The days passed and Amy played in the garden and happily swung on her swing. She hadn't seen her little friend Twinkle but she was there in Amy's mind a lot. She was still remembering her happy day at the bottom of the garden in the glade with Twinkle and all the animals, as she sat there swinging to and fro.

Suddenly, in her shimmering pink dress, Twinkle appeared! She asked Amy what she was thinking about, and Amy replied, "I was thinking about the day in the glade when I was so happy with you and all the animals!"

To her surprise Twinkle said, "You are a special little girl and I will come to you tonight, and because you are so special I will grant you a wish! So Amy, think very hard and tell me tonight what you would really like."

That day Amy was very quiet and thoughtful. She couldn't tell anyone why because no one would believe her, but very carefully she thought about her wish that Twinkle promised she would grant her. So when she went to bed that night she had a job to sleep because of the excitement and the wonder she felt.

After a long while Amy fell into a deep sleep and she was dreaming again when, suddenly, her room was filled with a wonderful glowing light and in the centre was Twinkle in her pink shimmering dress! Once again Amy rubbed her eyes and Twinkle spoke very softly to her to wake up.

Once Amy was fully awake Twinkle asked her if she was ready to ask her for her wish to be granted. After a long sigh, Amy said, "The one thing I would really like is that I will never really grow up and lose you, Twinkle, as my friend."

I think Twinkle must have granted her wish because to this day there is someone called Amy who really believes in fairies, and no one can convince her any different.